DEADLY PURPOSE
The High Sierras – Book 5

Diane Benefiel

PRAISE FOR DIANE BENEFIEL

Solitary Man

NATIONAL READERS' CHOICE AWARD WINNING NOVEL

"I am in love with this story. I devoured this book and didn't want it to end. The chemistry between the characters and the plot kept me wanting to read late into the night. This is my first read from Diane Benefiel but definitely not my last. I can't wait to read more from this amazing author. Thank you Diane Benefiel for getting me hooked on your books!" ~ CJ's Book Corner

"Ryder was exactly who Brenna needed in her life, and trust me when I say you will love him because yeah he really is that good of a guy. Solitary Man is my first book by this author and it will not be the last. I really think you all will enjoy this one as much as I did it is one I do recommend." ~ I'm A Sweet And Sassy Book Whore

"I really enjoyed this book and there were a few twists and turns that kept me completely involved in the story. This is the first time I have read this author and it definitely won't be my last!" ~ Sassy Southern Book Blog

HIGH SIERRAS SERIES

Flash Point

"Diane Benefiel takes us on a story filled with mystery, suspense, and action as we try to solve what is going on in the small town of Hangman's Loss. Flash Point is a story that will have you flipping the pages and wondering who is the behind the attacks against Hangman's newest resident and why." ~ Sarah Reads

*"**Flash Point** really surprised me. It's not what I was expecting but I really enjoyed reading it. It's a fun easy read that captured me from the start."* ~ Coffee Chat

Dead Giveaway

"Diane has written yet another winner in her High Sierra series. Murder witness and 'person of interest' Gwen flees with her godson to Cameron's uncle Eli. Gwen and Eli have no use for one another but come together for Cameron's sake and to find the true murderer...and in the process find their way to one another. My evening with Gwen and Eli couldn't have been more delightful, and I look forward to the next installment of the High Sierras." ~seniorphotog

*"I loved this second book in the High Sierras series. This is a story of two people who are attracted to each other, but reconnecting under the worst of circumstances. I discovered Ms. Benefiel's books and have loved the careful way she draws you in to the story with characters that make you feel as if you are reading about friends. I am really looking forward to the next High Sierras book, **Already Gone**."* ~paytonpuppy

Already Gone

"This series has only gotten better and better! Seriously, there's something that really speaks to my heart about Maddy and Logan, and Hangman's Loss FEELS like a small California town tucked away in the Sierras. They're such a power couple! I read this book in just a couple of days--totally sucked me in. It's that perfect blend of fun, sizzle, and suspense! I just want to live in Maddy's life forever but since I can't--I can't wait for the next book!" ~Katharine Montgomery

"A wonderful story about second chances. The minute you start reading, you will be instantly hooked. The author weaves a tale of drama and romance that keeps you enthralled and turning the pages. Maddie is feisty and Logan is her brooding and over protective suffering hero. The sparks fly every time they see each other. Eventually they give in and realize that they are perfect for each other and have always been. This is a great story right up to the last word." ~Simatsu

Burnover in Rescued Anthology

"Sweet, Sexy stories featuring furbabies and helping to save lives, it's a win win for all." ~Kara's Books

"8 stories by 8 outstanding authors. In these stories, there is a tattoo artist, two firefighters, two sheriff deputies, a famous furniture maker, a veterinarian, and a country music singer, and I loved them all. Then add in that each story has a dog or puppy that is rescued, along with a story of love and romance, it is a winning combination." ~Susan D

Boroughs
Publishing Group

www.BOROUGHSPUBLISHINGGROUP.com

DEADLY PURPOSE

ISBN 978-1-948029- 62-9

To my sisters, Ellen and Sandy, who share my memories of family vacations in the Sierras

ACKNOWLEDGMENTS

I want to acknowledge the guidance and support of Michelle Klayman at Boroughs Publishing Group, who not only is CEO of the company, but is now my editor. Michelle sold me on the idea of the High Sierras series and I couldn't be more grateful. Thanks, Michelle.

DEADLY PURPOSE

Chapter One

The shabby cabin should have looked dark and forlorn. Meg frowned, ignoring the throbbing behind her eyes, tightening her fingers on the steering wheel while the car engine idled and she tried to make sense of what she was seeing. Warm yellow light glowed from the windows, firewood lay neatly stacked on the porch, and a swirl of gray smoke rose from the chimney to dissipate into the tall pines towering overhead. A Thomas Kinkade painting come to life with the promise of home. But lighted windows and burning fireplaces in this particular cabin meant people, and her cabin should be empty.

On a sigh she pulled onto the driveway blanketed with pine needles and bordered by patches of dirty snow, frozen remnants of a storm from the not-too-distant past. The leaden clouds sinking over the pines looked heavy enough to drop from the sky. This cabin had been her Emerald City, the singular goal that had kept her going for the past week. If she could make it to the cabin, she'd be safe. If she could make it to the cabin, Julius would never find her. If she could make it to the cabin, she'd pull on her dad's old Pendleton shirt and curl up under the Hudson Bay blanket and feel again the unwavering but complicated love of her father.

But someone had beaten her to it. The cabin should look cold and dark, waiting for her to bring it to life. Instead, some trespasser had intruded into her space.

Turning off the engine, she considered what to do. Had she gotten turned around—somehow missed a road and ended up at the wrong house? She'd only been to the cabin a handful of times, but it had been longer than a dozen years, so it was possible she'd messed up the directions.

Surely the pitched metal roofs weren't unique. Lots of cabins had them to slough off winter snow. But she remembered the shed to the left that had housed a snowmobile, and the drive through the mountains from the town of Hangman's Loss was etched into her consciousness clearly from when she'd been that anxious young girl joining her father at the cabin for the first time.

She spied the hand-carved sign she'd made at Girl Scout camp when she was eleven, the one with little painted bears and squirrels circling the words "Welcome to Our Cabin." The memory of her father holding the nail (quite bravely, she realized now) while she'd used a hammer to tap it into the wood and hang the sign next to the door came back to her.

This was her cabin.

Forcing herself to move despite bone-deep achiness, she opened the car door. The warmth from the heater faded immediately in the frigid mountain air, and the shaky feeling that came with bone-deep chills she'd been experiencing returned with a vengeance. The plan had been to get to the cabin, get a fire started in the fireplace, then burrow under as many blankets as she could find until whatever bug she had caught passed. But maybe, like Dorothy on her way to the Emerald City, Meg had another challenge to overcome before reaching her goal. A glance at the sky indicated the clouds were even darker, obscuring the tops of the pines on the slope behind the cabin. She didn't know what snow clouds looked like, but with the seriously cold temperatures she'd probably find out soon enough.

Who was occupying her father's cabin? The mud showed furrows where a vehicle had driven around to the back. With a wary glance at the sky, she pulled a beanie out of her daypack and tugged it onto her head and followed the tracks. A mud-spattered, older-model Toyota 4Runner sat parked in the back. Damn, damn, damn. Why couldn't anything ever be simple?

She'd have to go to the door—should she use her key, unlock it, and walk right in or should she knock politely?—and ask what the hell the occupant was doing in her father's cabin. And get that person out as quickly as possible so she could crawl under those blankets before she passed out.

She dug down to try to find the old Meg, but the punishing past year on top of a bad case of she guessed the flu had knocked that woman out at the knees. The low burn of anger at having her sanctuary violated let her know kick-ass Meg wasn't dead; she'd only been taking a break. Squaring her shoulders, she stepped onto the porch, keys clutched in a tight grip. She'd start off nice and see what happened. She raised her fist to knock, then jerked back when the door swung open before her knuckles could connect.

The surly face of a bearded man was not what she expected. Tall and long-limbed, his wide shoulders filled the door. Furrowed brows shadowing dark brown eyes and a scowling expression did nothing to alleviate the feeling that she'd awakened a bear in its den. And a hungry bear at that.

"What do you want?"

About the same time he growled out the question, the warmth hit her. It emanated from inside the cabin and felt like a thick blanket pulled fresh from the dryer and wrapped snugly around her. She wanted to slip past him and find a place to lie down for the next week or so. Someplace out of the way where she could ignore him until she felt better and could deal with his intrusion.

He stepped forward and wariness had her taking a step back before she recovered herself. *Grow a spine. Don't cower. Stand up for yourself.*

He stepped onto the porch and pulled the door shut behind him.

Meg suppressed a groan at the loss of warmth. Gathering her resolve, she asked, "Who are you?" At least her voice sounded strong. "And what are you doing in my cabin?"

"Not your cabin. You must have missed a turn. Go figure out where." He reached back to lay a hand on the doorknob.

"This is my cabin. *You* need to leave."

He gave her a once-over before locking his gaze on hers. "I know what the owner of this place looks like, and you don't fit the bill. Go away."

"If I go away, I'll get the sheriff and let him deal with you. I don't think he'll tolerate squatters in these mountains. I'll give you ten minutes to get your things around, then you're gone."

"Go for it, lady. We have a police chief, not a sheriff, and cell coverage is spotty up here. By the time you get into town, it'll be dark. Chief Gallagher is too smart to bother with this right now. He'll tell you to get a room at a motel somewhere and figure it out in the morning."

She sized up the man. With his tough build, he wouldn't be easy to budge. This was not how she envisioned her day ending. She tightened her arms around her middle to stop the shiver snaking up her spine. A glance out from under the porch showed fat snowflakes wafting softly from the sky. She'd never seen snow falling before. Watching the drift of hazy white made her head swim.

"What the hell?" She jerked back when strong hands gripped her elbows, backing up her breath in her lungs. "What are you doing? Let go."

"Then don't act like you're going to pass out."

"I'm not going to pass out." She pulled against his hold. "Hands off."

He released her, putting his hands up like he was calming an emotionally disturbed person. The headache brewing at her temples spiked.

"You on something?"

Either irritation made his voice gruff, or it was his natural tone. She gave her forehead a surreptitious rub, not bothering to verbalize a response.

"Look at me." He cast his gaze over her face. Only full, sensuous lips softened the rough planes of his face. He raised a hand and she backed up. A fuzzy sensation crowded at the edge of her brain, reminding Meg of when she'd suffered a concussion after being beaned in the head by a softball pitch.

"Steady there." He held up a finger. "Without moving your head, follow my finger with your eyes."

She looked him straight in the eye. "You know what you can do with that finger, don't you?"

Only the slight crinkling at the corner of his eyes gave her any indication that the comment had struck home. He laid the back of his hand against her forehead. She didn't jerk back this time, but it was a close call.

"You're not high, you're sick. Your skin is hot to the touch."

She probably did have a fever, but while her face felt flushed, the rest of her couldn't get warm. "Would you go away? I want my cabin."

"Not your cabin," he reiterated. Stepping back, he rested his hands on his hips, brows lowered, reluctance evident in the lines on his face. "You're less than twenty minutes from town. Get yourself a motel room. Take some Tylenol."

Where did that kind of self-assurance come from? Maybe she'd had been like that once. She'd find that woman again. But for now, this man wasn't budging and her energy was draining away with the setting sun. The reality of another night spent in her car made that little spark of happiness she'd felt when she'd arrived at the cabin fade like embers in a cold fireplace.

Not sure how much longer she could stay on her feet, she turned to step off the porch. Something wet touched her flushed face, blessedly cool. That's right, it was snowing. She opened the back hatch of her small SUV. The folded-up rear seats had given her space to stow her belongings on one side and sleep on the other. She was barely medium height and if she tucked up her legs in her sleeping bag, she could sleep, albeit not comfortably.

Sitting in the door opening, she bent forward to unlace her boots. A quick hand to the door jamb helped steady her when her head threatened to fall off her shoulders. Moving slow was the name of the game. Moving slow and not bending over.

"What the hell are you doing?"

The man did cranky really well. With focused effort, she brought her foot up to rest on the bumper so she could reach the laces more easily. She hoped the fading light was a result of the sun going down, not loss of consciousness. If she could sleep, maybe she could beat this flu. Sleeping in the cabin would be loads better, but she'd slept in her SUV for the past four nights. She could make it one more. Then tomorrow first thing she'd go in search of the chief of police he'd mentioned.

"Lady, tell me what you're doing."

She leaned her head against her upraised knee. "You win for tonight. You get the cabin. I'll sleep here and in the morning get the police chief." Except she couldn't get the police chief. She rubbed her forehead against her knee. How could she have forgotten? Law enforcement of any type had to be avoided, at least until she finished what needed to be done. Exhaustion spread like an insidious poison, dragging at her limbs until she was sure she was about to dissolve into a boneless heap. She'd figure out her next step tomorrow.

She untied the laces on the boot, pulled it off, and brought up her other foot, all the while conscious of Mister Broody watching her out of hooded eyes. Carefully, she placed her boots next to her sleeping bag and scooted back.

"Be a pal and close the hatch."

"You can't sleep out here."

"You're in my cabin and won't leave, so this is exactly where I'm sleeping."

"It's too cold to sleep in the car."

She pulled the beanie lower over her ears. "It's not so bad."

He swore ripely and Meg forced back the instinctive flinch. She'd dealt with unpredictable moods from men before and survived.

"Get out of the car."

She eyed him cautiously. "Ah, no."

He ran a hand over his thick beard, muttering a string of profanities. His dark beard was threaded with strands of silver, and she wondered what he looked like clean shaven. He heaved an aggrieved sigh. "Jesus Christ. Okay, you can sleep in the cabin."

"Where will you sleep?"

"In the cabin. You can have the couch."

"No. Thank you, but no." She reached up to grab the door.

"You'll freeze your ass out here." If nothing else, the absolute reluctance in his tone should have been an indicator that she would be safe with him.

"I've got a sleeping bag. I'll be fine." When she pulled on the hatch, he held it open with a raised hand. Snow dusted his dark hair and the shoulders of his heavy plaid shirt.

"You can't be serious. You're sick. It's fucking snowing. You can't spend the night out here."

"Right. Whatever." Giving in was a strategic withdrawal. Feeling like she was using the last of her strength, she tugged on her boots, not bothering to tie the laces, and grabbed her keys. She pushed out of the vehicle. "I'll leave."

"Damn it," he growled. "You're going to park on the side of the road somewhere, aren't you? God save me from stupid women."

"I am not a stupid woman."

"You are if you think you'll sleep in a car in freezing weather. That's how people die."

She raised her gaze to his. "Stupid women are the ones who spend the night in a cabin with a strange, angry man."

"Then get a motel in town."

"Can't do that."

He'd stepped back so she could push the rear hatch shut. With a hand on the side of the car she moved around to the driver's door. She tipped her head back and gazed up at the sky. If you stared hard enough, you could follow a single snowflake as it drifted from high above. "I've never seen it snow before. It's beautiful."

Note to self, tilting your head back when you have the flu is to be avoided. The world swam crazily, and she tried to focus once again on getting to the car door. The ripe oath muttered from behind her should have been a warning, because suddenly the world tipped even more as she was swept up in arms as strong and unyielding as the tall trees surrounding them.

Fear rose like vomit, choking her. Bucking, twisting, kicking, she fought to get free, her breath coming in jerky gasps. "Let me down," she snarled. She swung a tight fist to catch him with a solid clip to the jaw then jammed an elbow into his gut.

He let go, dropping her onto a heap of pine needles. "Shit. Hit me again and I will let you freeze to death."

She scrambled to her feet, holding on to the side of her car for balance. "I wouldn't have hit you if you hadn't grabbed me."

"Lady, I only grabbed you to save you from passing out and ending up on your ass. Guess you ended up there anyway."

"Keep your hands to yourself. I'll leave, but you can place a bet that I'll be back first thing in the morning, so you better start packing."

"You're sleeping in the damn cabin."

She spotted her keys in the dirt where they'd landed when he dropped her. She bent to retrieve them but he was quicker, swooping down to gather them up. He pressed the remote and the SUV gave its little chirp to let her now it was locked, then deposited the keys in the front pocket of the heavy canvas pants he wore.

"Give me my keys."

"No." He strode to the cabin. "Come inside."

Chapter Two

Indecision warred inside her cloudy brain. He could be a serial killer even now plotting to murder her, hack her body to bits, and bury her in the woods. Or he could be a grumpy squatter who didn't really want to bother with her, but had enough decency not to want her sleeping in her car when she was sick. The truth? She was hungry, exhausted, and had used up all of the reserves of gumption she possessed.

Damn it. She trailed him across the porch where he stood with the door open. She grabbed hold of the jamb when the warmth hit her once again. The combination of heat with the heady smell of something aromatic cooking were enough to make her knees wobble.

"There's the couch. You're sleeping there."

She looked in the direction he pointed. A long dark leather couch she didn't recognize stood in front of the fireplace where a blaze snapped behind a screen. The tiny bedroom where she'd slept those long-ago summers was upstairs, but maybe he thought she'd feel safer with a little distance between them. She dragged her gaze back to study the man, trying to gauge his character, his trustworthiness. He didn't have mean eyes. As if that meant anything. His sheer reluctance to accommodate her was another vote in his favor. But he might be a good actor. If he'd really wanted to entice her to stay with him, to cause her harm, wouldn't he have been, well, nicer? Or maybe this was his strategy all along—get her to trust him then take advantage.

Standing in the open doorway, she was aware of the life-saving heat escaping into the snowy dusk. The choice between the cozy warmth inside the cabin and subfreezing temperatures outside should have decided her. But she knew danger could hide behind eyes fortified by false concern. The man stood with lowered brows, thumb tucked into the front pocket of his pants. He looked irritated and put out. Anything else would have made her suspicious.

After being so careful, so cautious, for so many months, the idea of putting her faith in a strange man seemed unfathomably careless. But at that moment survival dictated she trust him, because if she didn't get someplace warm and get some food in her belly, what she hoped was only a routine bout of the flu could easily turn into something much more serious.

She opened her mouth to speak but found her teeth wanted to chatter. It seemed her body had to go through a process before she could be warm. She tightened her jaw and enunciated carefully. "Okay. I need to get some things out of the car, and then I'll try to stay out of your way."

"Tell me what you want."

Suddenly too exhausted to do anything else, she sighed, then answered through gritted teeth. "My sleeping bag, pillow, and big black bag."

"That's it?"

"Oh, and my daypack. It's on the passenger seat."

She watched him move to the door. Why was he being so...not kind...reluctantly accommodating, perhaps? No, that was too generous. He appeared way too surly for that. But regardless that he obviously didn't want her around, and didn't think the cabin was hers, he was willing to let her stay. Under that gruff exterior maybe he felt sorry for her.

When he closed the door behind him, she gazed around the cabin, little things triggering memories of her father. As the child of never-married parents, and her mother having sole custody and only allowing her to spend time with her father on rare occasions, Meg had always felt the short visits she'd had with her dad were special, especially because they were so limited. The two of them had packed as much as they could into those brief summer months when she'd joined him at the cabin.

Despite some subtle changes, the interior was the same. Stairs to the right led up to the loft, and she thought the rail looked new. The big stone fireplace with the solid walnut mantel and the rustic chair with green leather upholstery were the same. A movement caught her eye, and she spied a small calico cat curled on a round bed near the fireplace, licking a paw and rubbing it over her face. For some reason, the cat's presence was reassuring. The man didn't look like a cat person, but since he apparently was, how bad could he be? On the other hand, Hitler had loved dogs.

The kitchen took up the back left corner of the first floor, and was pretty sparsely equipped. She had baked chocolate chip cookies for her dad in the unpredictable oven. He'd eaten even the crispy, overcooked ones, saying he'd never tasted better. An accordion door on a track hid a stacked washer/dryer combo, and a Crock Pot sat on the counter, steam escaping from around the lid. The dining table piled with books and papers and an open laptop computer doubled as a workspace.

Memories of her father felt like ghosts from the past, and she fought against the pricking tears. Despite the sadness, there was something comforting about being where she'd been happy as a child.

The door swung open and her reluctant host dumped her sleeping bag, pillow, and pack on the couch, letting her black bag hit the floor with a thud. The keys landed on top of the pile. He must trust her not to rabbit, but she still was nowhere near ready to put her faith in him.

"Packing rocks in there?"

"No." She glanced at him hastily but his expression remained the same, somewhat aloof and slightly irritated. What if he'd looked inside? She was getting careless.

She moved to the couch and arranged the sleeping bag and pillow. The warmth from the fireplace and the achiness of being ill combined to sap her energy. With her boots set neatly at the end of the couch, it took all her reserves to slip inside and pull the bag up to her ears, sighing as she closed her eyes. The man hadn't moved. For all she knew he was still staring at her.

Meg didn't care.

She was finally starting to feel like maybe she wouldn't fall victim to hypothermia. Her head hurt, her bones ached, and she shivered occasionally, but feeling warm for the first time in what seemed like days made everything else fade in significance.

"Shit. You should have Tylenol."

Sleepiness slurred her reply.

"What?"

She put more effort into her words. "Crappy bedside manner. Hope you're not a nurse."

He snorted. She might have thought he was suppressing a laugh, but she couldn't imagine that grim face relaxing into humor.

"What's your name?"

She raised her eyelids enough to see the frown was still in place. "Meg. What's yours?"

After a long moment he replied, "Declan."

"Okay." Feeling oddly safe, she let sleep take her.

***

Dex sat in the chair by the fireplace, legs stretched in front of him. He rubbed his right thigh where a bone-deep ache reminded him he still wasn't one hundred percent healed. Not as bad as it had been, but still a nagging reminder of his former life. The cat wandered over and he scratched her ears when she jumped onto his lap.

The woman had checked out before he could get her to take anything for the fever. What the hell was he going to do with her? Who drove into the mountains when they were sick, and without a firm idea of where they were going? A check of the registration in the glove box had revealed her name, but he'd asked anyway, testing whether she'd be straight with him. Meghan Bennett, address in Santa Cruz. A quick look through the small SUV and it was obvious she'd been living out of her car.

There were no printouts from motels, and the receipts he'd found told him she'd bought a container of yogurt and a box of granola bars at a gas station in Sacramento, then a banana, protein bars, and a bottle of pain reliever along with gas in Truckee. All paid for with cash.

He rose and moved to the kitchen, the cat trotting in front of him. He dumped a couple spoonfuls of food from a can into her bowl, and once he'd filled his mug with coffee, he returned to the chair, iPad tucked under his arm. The iPad sat unused as he sipped the strong brew, watching the woman.

She was on the run, apparently without much in the way of resources. That she'd insisted the cabin was hers bothered him. She was wrong, and he'd need to move her along once she could stand without doing a face plant. But something about that felt off. She'd sure as hell acted sincere. Regardless, he damn sure didn't want to get involved in someone else's drama.

For the most part, he'd managed to avoid people for the past year or so. He'd come up to the mountains to clear his head. Let his leg heal. Lick his wounds, if he was honest. Solitude worked best for him. Solitude and physical labor. He'd rebuilt the supports for the sagging porch. Replaced the handrail along the stairs to the loft. Refinished the cabinet faces in the kitchen and bathroom. And in the last couple months he'd finally begun sleeping better.

He'd even worked up the enthusiasm to go hiking to some of the lakes that dotted the mountain slopes rising above the town. He hadn't gone far, and his bum leg kept the hikes on the moderate side, but he'd done it. That he'd also managed to get a couple hundred pages of his new book written into the laptop had surprised him because he didn't suck at writing as much as he'd once feared he would.

Being in the mountains felt like a balm to his soul. He didn't know if there was any place more beautiful than the Eastern Sierras. Hangman's Loss was miniscule compared to the city he'd come from, but the town had enough of the necessities so far that he hadn't needed to look elsewhere for anything. The people were decent, and he could admit to himself that getting corralled into helping Chief Gallagher and the FBI with a police investigation a while back had been a welcome diversion—one that had allowed him to close an aspect of his life with a satisfying ending.

From that he'd somehow made a few friends, men and women he liked and who mercifully left him alone for the most part. If he ventured into town, it was usually to hit the grocery store or the building supply place and then come straight back to the cabin. He was still working himself up to the point where he'd actually accept one of the invitations to hang out, maybe spend an evening at the pub in town.

He studied what he could see of the woman's features. Meghan Bennett was attractive, and would probably tick that up a few notches to striking when she wasn't sick and underweight. For a moment there he'd had her in his arms, so he knew she couldn't weigh more than one ten, tops. Her hair remained hidden under the beanie, but given the sooty lashes and brows, he guessed dark. The eyes were a deep, mysterious blue. At the moment, the lashes lay across cheeks so pale they looked nearly translucent.

The sky darkened outside the windows as night fell, and he rose to pull the curtains closed and throw another log into the fire. He stood beside her, watching her sleep, and told himself emphatically she wasn't his problem.

***

Meg blinked open her eyes and took a minute to focus. To gather her thoughts. The cabin. She was at her dad's cabin. She sat up slowly, wincing as her muscles protested. She fingered the woolen blanket draped over the sleeping bag. It was the Hudson Bay blanket that had covered her bed as a child, cream colored and with its distinctive stripes. A small bottle of Tylenol and a glass of water sat on the coffee table.

She froze when she saw the man sitting in the chair, dark eyes focused on her.

Meg held his gaze for a long moment, decidedly uncomfortable to find he'd tended to her while she slept. A blanket, pain meds. It wasn't only the odd intimacy, but the fact that she hadn't awoken when he'd gotten that close.

She cleared her throat. "I'm sorry, I don't remember your name."

"Declan."

"Right. Declan." Unusual name, she thought, wondering if he was Irish. She glanced to the windows. Through the narrow slit in the curtains she could see the blackness of night. "What time is it?"

"After seven. You've been asleep over two hours."

"Wow. Okay." She shifted to sit up and swung her feet to the floor. "Excuse me."

She rose slowly, and when her legs remained steady, made her way to the door tucked under the staircase. Even moving carefully every muscle in her body reminded her the battle against the flu had yet to be won.

The door opened to the bathroom, looking better maintained than she remembered. Her father's habit had been to let things go until they absolutely had to be dealt with or risk falling apart. Minutes later she returned to the living room and found the man, *Declan*, she reminded herself, had placed a wide-brimmed soup mug on the coffee table, steam rising from its surface. A spoon rested beside it.

He stood beside the fireplace, arms crossed in front of him. She was beginning to suspect the frown was habitual.

"What's that?"

"Stew. Eat it."

It smelled amazing, rich and fragrant, but she absolutely *hated* accepting help from anyone. "I have my own food."

"Like what?"

The question surprised her only because she hadn't expected him to ask. He'd been so gruff before, so adamant she didn't belong here. Added to the blanket he must have thrown over her sleeping bag, checking to make sure she had food almost felt like he cared. And she was an idiot if she was looking for caring from a stranger.

She reached over and unzipped the side pocket of her black bag. Fishing inside, her fingers brushed the smooth leather of the holster and the cold metal of the Colt .45 pistol before wrapping around plastic packaging. She pulled out the Kind bar and zipped the bag closed, then held it up. "This."

Shaking his head, he said, "Eat the soup."

With that order firmly stated, he crossed the room to the kitchen, leaving her on her own. She decided refusing the stew when it smelled so good really did make her a stupid woman. She picked up the spoon and mug and stirred the contents with an appreciative sniff. Beef stew with lots of broth and chunks of meat and vegetables. He'd used elbow pasta instead of potatoes. Yum.

She tucked her feet under her and pulled the blanket over her lap as she leaned against the back of the couch, clutching the mug. She sipped the broth, then spooned up peas and a bite of meat. God, was there anything as comforting as sitting in front of a fireplace and eating steaming beef stew on a cold, snowy evening? She swallowed and felt the warmth spread from her belly outward. Another few bites and her headache eased a fraction.

Declan returned carrying his own mug, the cat trailing behind him. He set the mug on a little table beside the chair, then stooped to open the screen and throw a log onto the grate in the fireplace. The fire sparked and bright flames began hungrily devouring the new fuel. He sat down and rested his forearms on his knees, gaze steady.

"You know this place."

"Sure. I told you this is my cabin." That cat jumped onto the couch and settled next to her, so Meg stretched out a hand to stroke her head.

"It's not your cabin, but it's clear you've been here before." When she stared at him, he added, "The bathroom isn't in an obvious location but you knew exactly where to go."

She rubbed her forehead with a closed fist, avoiding the bruised area. Despite the nap, exhaustion dragged, making her feel like her brain synapses were firing through sludge. "Yep, I did." Finished with her stew, she set down the mug.

"Damn it, you're almost asleep again. We'll talk tomorrow."

"Good plan," she muttered.

Pills rattling in the medicine bottle roused her.

"Take these before you pass out." He held out his hand, two oblong Tylenol tablets resting on his wide palm. She took the pills and he handed her the glass of water.

"You're not really that grouchy."

He didn't say anything until after she swallowed the pills. "Look, there's an extra toothbrush in the medicine cabinet if you want to use it."

"I have my own toothbrush." She pushed back on the fatigue and rose from the couch. "I'll brush my teeth and then be out of your way." She unzipped her bag and grabbed what she needed. In the bathroom, she tugged off the beanie and changed into the sweatpants and long-sleeved t-shirt she used as pajamas. She brushed, then rinsed the toothpaste from her mouth, trying to convince herself not to overthink this. For some reason, she felt safe with Declan and didn't get any weird vibes. She'd trust her instincts and deal with cabin ownership when she felt better in the morning.

Meg splashed water on her face and eyed her reflection in the mirror as she dabbed her face with a towel. The woman staring back at her looked too thin, and undeniably pale. She fluffed her short hair with her fingers. Cutting her hair in that gas station bathroom had altered her looks, made her eyes appear bigger, her neck longer. The change in appearance probably wouldn't fool anyone, but it had seemed prudent at the time.

Had it only been one week ago when she'd finally decided she couldn't put off implementing her plan any longer? Careful preparation had paid off. A successful escape had depended on paying attention to every tiny detail, not leaving any evidence that could make Julius suspicious. Only her mother, Sarah, had known of her plan. She hadn't liked it, but had finally, reluctantly acquiesced. She had bought the sleeping bag and kept the gun for Meg, until the day she was ready to leave.

The day she ran, she'd managed to transfer one hundred fifty thousand dollars. That had only been a small portion of the whole amount, but it had brought the total disbursements to over seven hundred eighty thousand dollars. Her laptop was in her bag. As soon as she could manage, she'd transfer the rest of the money, and by then the risk of Julius finding her through online activity would be neutralized, because once it was done she'd be ready to go to a law enforcement agency that might actually do something.

It would be hard for him to get to her if she was sitting in a jail cell.

Good would come from the bad—she was making sure of it. She'd downloaded the last of the files from his computer, and she needed some time to go through them. If what she thought she'd discovered was correct, there was likely enough evidence on that flash drive to put him in prison for a long time. She needed a couple more days, time to examine the files and disburse the rest of the money. She adjusted the chain holding the flash drive around her neck, moving it under the collar of her shirt.

She hadn't planned on leaving on the night she'd fled, but Julius's behavior had become increasingly erratic. One day he'd be elated, over the moon, stoked because the planned expansion into the big Asian markets was taking off, or the book was going well, or whatever else he deemed positive had happened. Then the next day he'd be in the depths of despair, sure he was going to fail, and taking his frustration out on Meg. Yelling, screaming, blaming her.

The afternoon she'd left he'd had a meeting with a backer he desperately needed if he was going to hook other investors. That he'd failed was immediately apparent when he walked through the front door of the house, picked up the beautiful ceramic bowl off the side table, and hurled it against the stone fireplace where it shattered into thousands of brightly colored shards.

Now only her mother knew where Meg was, because only Sarah Bennett could be trusted.

Meg wished she knew what was happening. She'd slipped sedatives into Julius's beer and had escaped when he'd fallen asleep. But what if she'd used too many? What if the combination of alcohol and Diazepam had been too much? What if she'd killed him? It was more than possible the police were looking for her. If she had access to the Internet, she could find out what was going on.

Gathering up her toiletries, she left the bathroom and returned to the couch. As much as she wished to talk to her mother, calling Sarah was too risky. Emailing her was also risky. Meg would stick to the schedule—at the ten-day mark she would use the burner phone and check in, let her mother know she was okay, and find out what had been reported in the Santa Cruz papers.

Snuggled into her sleeping bag, she watched Declan standing at the sink in the tiny kitchen, scrubbing a pot with soapy hands. *A man who does dishes.* For some reason that gave her a tingly feeling in her belly. Maybe it was the contrasts—a broad-shouldered guy with the sleeves of his heavy flannel shirt rolled up to the elbows, the muscles of his arms cording as he turned the pot under the running water while he had a dishtowel draped over his shoulder.

The fact that she found him undeniably sexy was a surprise and a warning. Getting involved with anyone at this point in her life was insane. But that didn't mean she couldn't enjoy the view.

Soup and a couple of painkillers must really be a wonder cure because she felt better than she had in a long time.

Chapter Three

Dex squirted dish soap into the basin and resigned himself to the mindlessness of the chore. Cooking didn't bother him mostly because he liked to eat good food, but he really disliked cleanup duty. But he refused to put it off. If he cooked, then every damn spoon and pan got washed and put away so the task wasn't hanging over his head. He didn't bother wishing for a dishwasher.

Thoughts of the woman sleeping on his couch wouldn't leave him alone. What was he going to do with her? She was on the run, and experience told him a woman on the run likely had an abusive husband or boyfriend in her past. And since on the run meant fear of pursuit, he'd keep an eye out for as long as she was with him.

Dumping the soapy water and giving the countertops a wipe, he considered his options. He could go to Brad Gallagher, get the police chief to run a background check on her, see what popped. But he might as well take out a banner ad in the newspaper proclaiming she'd ended up on his doorstep. Regardless, first things first. She needed to get over whatever virus she had, then they'd see what's next.

He moved to the window and peered out. Didn't matter what he wanted anyway; the early-season storm was dumping snow by the plowful, and by morning there'd be a foot or more, making the roads impassable. And more snow was forecast for tomorrow. Like it or not, he was stuck with his houseguest for the next little while.

A glance at the couch told him Meghan was either sleeping or giving a good imitation of it. He pushed aside a stack of books and sat at the dining table, then opened the email app on his iPad. A message from his mother almost had him cracking a smile. She wanted him to weigh in about whether she and his stepfather should go on an expedition to Antarctica (her bucket list included setting foot on all seven continents) or hike a long segment of the Pacific Crest Trail, with the goal of working up to doing the whole thing start to finish at some point. He tapped out a short reply.

Do the PCT—I'll join you for a few days when you get to my mountains. Antarctica is for wimps. Save it for when you're old.

Having turned seventy a month before, she'd like that one.

Forty minutes later, he'd paid a couple bills, ignored the emails from friends back in Los Angeles, and begun poking around into Meghan Bennett's life. After several clicks he found a website, then let out a careful breath when the posted photo gave him an unwanted jolt. Long, wavy black hair, eyes a dark indigo blue glowing from under winged brows, and skin porcelain fair with the hint of peach in her cheeks. The angle of her head, the tilt of her chin, portrayed confidence and intelligence. The image of the woman on the screen was fucking gorgeous. He glanced at the slight form on the couch. She'd thrown off the covers and lay on her back, one arm flung above her head. Her sweatshirt had hitched up to show a scant few inches of pale skin, from the dip of her navel to the flare of her hip. He forced his gaze away.

Meghan Bennett was a writer, and from the samples on the website, she had talent, real talent. The site identified her genre as young adult. She had written a series called The Darkening of Ardenstal that looked like an epic fantasy with elves, wizards, and dragons. And a kick-ass heroine. The poise she exuded through her website didn't mesh with the vulnerable, fragile woman he'd been worried might keel over at his feet.

The clock said past ten when he clicked off the iPad and sat watching her in the flickering light from the fireplace. He'd draped an extra blanket over her earlier because she'd seemed so damned cold, and had been relieved that she hadn't woken to catch him in the act.

Now he rose to adjust the thermostat higher than he would if it were only him, laid more logs on the fire, then crossed the braided rug to the end table. He reached under the shade to turn off the lamp and found himself pausing to study her. The soft light showed she'd shifted to lie on her side, curled into herself in a pose that looked defensive. The beanie had come off and revealed that the long hair in the photo on her website had been ruthlessly chopped. He frowned, tilted the lamp closer, and bent over to peer at the smudge of purplish yellow shadowing her temple.

He straightened abruptly. She'd been hit. He beat back the flash of rage spiking through him, his fists clenched at the impotence he always felt when confronted with physical abuse. How many times had he wanted to pound in some dickhead's face, but instead had to quietly urge the woman to press charges, assuring her that they'd do their best to protect her. The memory of a Madonna-like face, upper lip split and bleeding, and the dark-eyed little girl clutching her skirt, both watching him with that wary, wounded doe look, crept in. Then the mother had taken that baby back into the apartment, closing herself inside with the monster. Three days later she was dead, and he'd had to hold the hysterical child who'd witnessed what no child ever should.

Meg stirred restlessly, making breathless, fearful sounds. A nightmare. He stepped back, reminding himself that years on the force, and his own personal relationships, had taught him that more often than not, caring about people usually came back to bite him, one way or another.

***

He'd found her. A noise, quiet in the half light, gave him away. Julius was here, unseen but close. Even as she told herself not to be afraid, that she could protect herself, the terror made its way through a tiny chink in her armor of resolve. She could get away. Once she was in a safe place, she'd make a new plan. Even as she thought it, he appeared, holding a woman from behind, an arm tight around her neck. It looked like her mother, but peering closer, she saw her own features, eyes bulging, mouth opening and closing in a desperate attempt for air. And in that moment she was there, in that hold, his breath hot and sour on the side of her face. "You always knew it would end this way. You should never have taken that money. I want it back, and I want the files back. People who double-cross me die."

Kicking back, she struggled against his hold while fighting to suck air into her lungs. *The gun.* The gun her father had given her that her mother had kept for her. She reached behind her back to the waistband of her jeans and the cold metal slipped comfortingly into her hand.

She blinked to clear her vision. Where was she? They'd been outside on the deck, the fog from the ocean hanging damp in the air, but now she was in a shadowed room, a soft light coming from behind her. She tightened her grip on the .45.

"What the fuck?"

The tall, broad-shouldered man stood over her, hands raised in front of him. Not Julius.

"You want to point that someplace else?" Eyes iron-hard stared out from under heavy brows. Declan. The flood of relief made her head swim. The dream had seemed so real. The arm around her neck, the struggle for air. But the man in front of her was not Julius. Still, he'd been standing over her while she slept.

Despite her pulse pounding in her ears so loud she could hardly hear over it, she didn't waver, keeping the muzzle of the gun aimed center mass. "What are you doing?"

A log on the grate snapped, a loud crack in the quiet. She reflexively glanced toward the fireplace and it took only that second of distraction and he wrenched the gun from her hold. Her stomach sank as, with quick, practiced moves, he ejected the clip and pulled back the slide to dispel the bullet in the chamber. Pocketing the ammunition, he held the gun at his side.

"Any more ammo in that bag?"

"Give me back my gun."

"Hell no."

"It's mine, you have no right to take it."

"You pointed it at me with your finger on the trigger. I have every damn right." He moved to set the pistol on the mantel, and when he returned, he grasped the handles of her black bag. He turned on another lamp and proceeded to unzip the bag and the side pockets and upend the contents onto the coffee table, scattering her belongings.

"Hey. Stop. What are you doing?" Meg grabbed her laptop before it could slide to the floor. She scrambled forward and scooped up the silky underwear and box of tampons mixed with cotton shirts and jeans.

He didn't respond, instead snagging her daypack and following the same procedure. "Checking to be sure you can't rearm yourself. Self-preservation is pretty important to me. I don't like looking down the business end of a gun."

It suddenly hit her what she'd done. Burying her face in a thin t-shirt wadded up in her hands, she let go a ragged sigh. "Sorry. It was a bad dream."

He shoved her belongings aside to sit on the coffee table, knees bumping hers. She pressed back against the sofa cushion. She didn't like that he was so much bigger than her. His imposing presence made her feel hemmed in, crowded. She closed her eyes rather than look at him.

"Tell me what's going on."

The low voice held a seductive quality that made her want to trust him. The urge to share her burden, to let him shoulder some of it, was so overwhelming the words were on the tip of her tongue before she forced them back.

"No." She opened her eyes to find his expression hardening behind the beard.

"You're in danger or you wouldn't be sleeping with a loaded gun under your pillow. I can't protect you unless I know where the threat is coming from."

"Give me back my forty-five and ammunition and I can protect myself."

"Lady, you were about ready to shoot me. I'm going to hold on to the gun for now."

"Right. Sorry." With the adrenaline spike waning, fatigue and depression dragged at her with dull claws. She stifled a sigh. "Okay, then why were you standing over me?"

He leaned forward and used a long forefinger to lift the short curls from her temple. "Quite a bruise you've got there. Want to tell me how you got it?"

She pulled away from his touch. "No. And that doesn't answer my question."

He shrugged. "I was turning off the lamp and you were twitching and muttering. I noticed the bruise. Makes me fucking crazy when I see women who have been hit."

"Seen a lot of them?"

"Enough. Tell me what happened." He held up a finger when she opened her mouth to speak. "And 'no' isn't going to cut it this time."

"I don't have to tell you anything."

His face may have been impassive, but his eyes held a tangible compassion that she felt as surely as a physical touch.

She held his gaze and felt the warmth low in her belly ratchet up a notch, a warmth that had nothing to do with the heat emanating from the fireplace. As hard and gruff as this man appeared, he possessed an innate kindness under his rough exterior. But tempting as it was to dump her problems at his feet, she couldn't let herself be drawn in. She had to get him out of her cabin so she could deal with whatever came at her on her own. Simply being around her put him in danger.

"If trouble is going to follow you to my doorstep, I want to be prepared."

She shook her head. "It's my doorstep, and once you're gone, not your problem."

He drummed his fingers on his knee, then gave a curt nod and rose abruptly. A moment later his firm tread sounded on the stairs. He didn't even bother to take the gun with him. He had all her ammo.

She took a moment to repack her things, placing the bags zipped and ready beside the couch in case she needed to grab them and go. Curling up inside her sleeping bag once again, she let herself drift. Of its own volition, her mind settled on images of the man upstairs, a man she thought could be dangerous if given the right incentive. Which struck her as odd given that even with him pissed off at her, she felt safer knowing he slept in the loft above her than she had with the gun tucked under her pillow.

***

Meg sat up and stretched, pausing to take stock. Muscles still ached, but not as bad. The headache was gone. Best of all, she'd slept soundly for the first time in months. She brought up her hand to push back the hair on her face, and was surprised to feel the short curls.

It occurred to her that there was an unnatural quiet in the cabin. In those long-ago summers she'd spent here with her father, her most vivid memories included waking to the sound of Steller's jays, the quiet rush of Coldwater Creek as it made its way to the lake, and the whisper of the wind in the pines.

The half-light of early morning showed through a narrow gap in the curtains. Stepping into her boots, she crossed to a window and pulled aside the paisley material. What she saw had her rushing to throw open the front door, then she stood there, holding her breath. Snow blanketed everything. The rounded shape of her car looked like an Eskimo's igloo. Branches of the tall pine trees sagged under the weight of the snowfall. She stepped out from under the porch and reached up to pull a branch closer. Snowflakes clung in individual, sparkling crystals. She gazed upward. Rose-tinted clouds glowed to the east, leaving the rest of the sky scrubbed clear by the storm.

Bending down, she scooped up a handful of snow, then gave in to the temptation to taste it with the tip of her tongue. Hmm, well, ice was ice. She packed the snow into a ball. Looking around for a good target, she stopped short at the sight of the tall, bearded man in many-pocketed cargo pants leaning against a post on the porch, the cat sitting regally next to him.

She jiggled the snowball, and he narrowed his eyes. "I wouldn't."

She giggled, surprising herself with the happy sound. "I've never had a snowball fight."

"Well, you're not having one now."

Her hands were starting to freeze so she hurled the snowball at a tree trunk. "Spoilsport." She gave a shiver as the icy breeze picked up.

"Right. You done playing in the snow?"

"Maybe."

She mounted the steps to the porch and found herself stopping in front of him, that dark gaze holding hers. He raised a hand and stroked the back of a long finger down one cheek. When she sucked in a breath, he murmured, "Fever is gone."

The heat in her belly, the surge in her heart rate, were warning enough that she needed to take a step back. A giant step. Mentally, as well as literally. He didn't smile and his expression remained serious. He turned and Meg followed him into the cabin.

***

Head tilted back under the showerhead, Meg let hot water sluice over her body. A body that hadn't felt this attracted to a man in a long time. She and Declan were circling around, each eyeing the other warily. Attraction simmered, at least on her part. He, on the other hand, didn't give much away.

She poured shampoo into her palm, setting the tiny bottle back on the shelf next to the taller black bottle of guy shampoo. She worked up a lather, then began rinsing. Once she'd showered, they'd need to talk. The cabin had belonged to her father. She'd inherited it, but had yet to have the title transferred. And, added bonus, she'd never mentioned the cabin to Julius. With her new short hair rinsed clean and conditioned, she twisted off the taps and wrapped a towel around her sarong-style, then stepped out of the shower.

She caught her reflection in the mirror. Thankfully her cheeks held a bit more color so she didn't look quite so waifish. She lifted the damp bangs. The bruise Declan had noticed had faded to less purple and more green. Julius had slipped up, giving her the impetus to leave.

She toweled off and dressed, not even bothering to wish for a hairdryer or styling product. She fluffed her curls the best she could before gathering her things and stepping out of the bathroom.

Declan sat at the small dining table, tapping on a laptop. Books and papers that had been on the table now sat piled on a chair against the wall. He glanced up when she hesitated next to the sofa.

"Coffee?" he asked. She nodded and he pointed toward the kitchen. "It's brewed."

She opened a cupboard and retrieved a mug. The sugar was still in the metal tin under the counter and she added a heaping spoonful before pouring in the coffee. She pulled a protein bar from her pocket as she sat across from him.

He frowned, returning to his habitually solemn expression. She wondered how he'd look if he actually smiled.

"You want cereal or toast or something?"

She shook her head and unwrapped the bar. Given the rinsed bowl and spoon on the counter, she guessed he'd opted for cereal.

The cat leapt onto her lap and kneaded its claws into her thigh, then settled into a furry ball. Charmed by the light purring, Meg stroked the soft head. "What's your cat's name?"

"She's not my cat, and her name is BC."

Still stroking the warm fur, she said, "She sure seems to think she's your cat. And what does BC stand for?"

"She's my niece's cat, and BC stands for Buttercup."

"So why don't you call her Buttercup?"

He gave her a look and she smothered a laugh. "Oh, I see. Buttercup is too sweet a name for you to use."

"Buttercup is a six-year-old's name for a cat. There's no dignity in it."

"Hmm." She bit off another chunk of her bar, chewing thoughtfully. They might as well get to it. "How come you're in my cabin?"

"How come you think it's your cabin?"

She swallowed, then said, "I inherited this cabin from my father. I'll do the paperwork to put my name on the title soon. And don't try to tell me I've got the wrong place. There's a sign outside the front door I made in Girl Scouts, and you noticed and commented that I know where the bathroom is. This is my cabin."

"What's your father's name?"

"Roy Evans."

He froze with his coffee mug halfway to his mouth. He lowered it slowly back onto the table. "Roy Evans is dead?"

"Yes."

"When?"

"Two months ago."

His expression tightened, and he stared blankly past her for a long minute. "Son of a bitch."

Chapter Four

"I'm sorry." The gruff emotion in his voice had her staring at him with curiosity. "Roy Evans was a good man."

"Yes, he was. You knew him?"

He lifted the cup and sipped his coffee before speaking. "You could say that."

When he didn't explain, she rolled her eyes. "Jeez, loosen up, will you? How did you know my dad?"

"Your dad and mine were in the Marine Corps and served together in Vietnam. Roy saved my dad's life during the Easter Offensive in seventy-two." Dark eyes watched her over the rim of the mug. "Any of that sound familiar?"

Meg shook her head.

"They kept touch sporadically after the war. I first met Roy when I was twenty-one."

Because she knew so little of her father's life, Meg had always hoarded the bits of information she did have. She'd known he'd served in the Marine Corps during the Vietnam War, but the Easter Offensive? She'd never heard of it. She filed away the new knowledge to be brought out later and examined. "That's it?"

He studied her, and she wondered if he was looking for a resemblance to her father. He tapped his fingers on the table, the frown back in place. His expression made her think he was carefully picking his words, making her wonder what he didn't want to reveal. "A year or so ago, I went to see him at that place where he was living in Santa Cruz. Can't say he was happy, but he seemed content."

"I hope he was."

"He mentioned he'd reconnected with his daughter. Said he'd been a shitty father, and was glad you'd forgiven him."

Carefully, she untwined her fingers. "I understood more of why he was so difficult to get along with after he was diagnosed with PTSD. When I was little, all I knew was that my dad wasn't around. He was a lot older than my mom, almost twenty years. I don't think he ever expected to have a kid. We lived in the Bay area, he lived in Los Angeles. But he came up here during his vacations, and from the time I was around nine until I was out of high school, I spent part of each summer with him."

"He said his daughter was paying for the facility he was in."

"Most of it was covered by his pension, but the rest I paid for. Regardless, you haven't explained how you ended up at his cabin."

He leaned back in his chair, tapping his fingers on the table. "Right. I quit my job, needed to get my head together." There was a long pause, and Meg had the feeling there was a whole book in what he wasn't saying.

"I hadn't talked to Roy in years, then out of the blue he calls. He was sick, so maybe it was his way of saying good-bye. Somehow we talked for an hour. He wanted me to stay at the cabin. Said the mountains would bring me peace, like they'd done for him, or some such shit." He raised his shoulders in a shrug that for some reason made him look lonely. "Plus," he continued, "he didn't like leaving the place unoccupied. I wanted to pay rent but he wouldn't take my money. We worked it out that I'd take care of whatever maintenance needed doing, and we'd call it even." He gave her his direct look. "How come your last name's not Evans?"

"How do you know it's not?"

"I looked on your car registration."

Not sure how she felt about that, she answered him. "Bennett is my mom's last name. My parents never married."

His fingers stopped their tapping, and his next question caught her off guard. "What are you running from?"

She responded carefully. "What makes you think I'm running from anything?"

"You've been living out of your car. The receipts in your glovebox show you've been paying cash for food and fuel. You've got a bruise on your forehead, and you're so jumpy you drew down on me."

Her stomach dropped as the markers fell in place. The practiced moves, the questions, the way he carried himself, all now made sense. "Damn. You're a cop."

His expression didn't change.

"I'm right, aren't I? You're a cop, like my dad."

"Used to be. Not anymore."

She lurched to her feet, crossing to the sofa in the living room. Quickly, she rolled her sleeping bag, then began stuffing her belongings into her duffel.

"Hold on." He came to stand across the coffee table from where she zipped the black bag closed with jerky movements. She crossed to the mantel and grabbed the .45 and stuffed it inside with everything else. "I want my ammo clip back."

"No."

She stared at him for a long minute, then whirled to the staircase. He'd taken the clip with him when he'd gone upstairs the night before. There was so much anger in her, her insides were shaking. Anger at herself for trusting him, for thinking she was safe to stay in the cabin with a stranger. She should have stuck with the lesson she'd learned long ago—trusting someone was asking to be taken advantage of.

She'd loved her father, but he'd never been someone who was *there* for her, whom she could rely on. There'd been that disastrous relationship in college, then another that had ended eighteen months ago when she'd discovered she and the guy had quite different understandings of exclusive, since his had included hooking up with his ex.

Her mother had been her rock, the one constant in her life. Her experiences with men, though, should have made her warier of Julius. Trusting him had turned into an utter disaster. What had started as her dream job had transformed into a situation that was not only dangerous, but that would in all likelihood result in her arrest. Lesson learned. Relying on herself was the only sure thing in life.

She pounded up the stairs to the loft, the sound of a heavy tread following her as she crossed the miniscule landing to the larger bedroom. She started with the nightstand, yanking open the drawer, pushing aside an unopened box of condoms, a couple of paperback novels, a book of crossword puzzles. "Excellent, you practice safe sex. Very smart. And crossword puzzles are good for your brain."

Declan leaned against the door jamb regarding her with that steady dark gaze.

Next she tried the dresser, opening drawers, pushing aside socks, boxer shorts, t-shirts. She knelt to tug open the bottom drawer, then sat motionless. She recognized defeat when it stared her in the face. A black metal gun locker with a complicated-looking lock sat next to folded sweatshirts. It might as well have been a bank vault.

She stood to face him, crossing her arms in front of her to keep from giving in to the urge to pummel him senseless.

"I need my clip, then I'll leave. You can forget you ever saw me."

"Not likely."

Not sure what he meant by that, she looked away, taking in her father's old room that was now Declan's. A photo showing a family with big smiles all around stood framed on the dresser. Whoever they were, Declan wasn't the guy with the attractive wife and sweet-looking kids. Books crowded the shelves of the simple bookcase and looked like the same titles she and her dad had read together all those years ago. *The Yearling, The Last of the Mohicans, Understood Betsy*—books that had shaped her career path.

"Declan what?"

When she caught the raised brow, she elaborated. "Your last name—Declan what?"

"Murphy."

"Middle name?"

"Michael."

Definitely Irish. "Okay, Declan Michael Murphy, I want my clip back. I'm not staying here with a cop." She frowned. "You knew my dad was a cop?"

He nodded. "Tell me what you're running from."

"Why? Are you going to rescue me? Protect me from my own personal bogeyman?"

"No." He ran a hand over his beard. "I think you can probably take care of yourself when you're not about to do a faceplant because you're sick. But if someone is after you, if you need help, you should see Chief Gallagher. He'll be straight with you."

Her brief laugh held no amusement. "I'm not spilling my guts to a cop. I tried that before and nothing good came of it. I dug myself a hole and I have to get out of it without bringing anyone else down with me." She rose to her feet, mind flitting from option to option, trying to assess all the variables, to figure out a way to stay safe. And how to stay out of jail long enough to finish disbursing the money.

"Regardless, you're staying put until the roads are plowed."

Crap. She'd forgotten about the snow. Meg paused at the door. "When will that be?"

"This far from town, and with more snow on the way? Not today."

Meg crossed to the window to pull back the curtain. Where the sky had been clear an hour earlier, clouds were again crowding over the mountains. Damn. Declan should be the one leaving, not her. Could her luck get any worse? Not only was her cabin, her refuge, occupied by an unwanted intruder, but the guy was a cop. It didn't matter that he wasn't still in law enforcement. That mind-set didn't change just because he'd stopped wearing a badge.

Declan disappeared and the sound of his footsteps receded down the stairs. Meg dropped onto the bed, fingering the old patchwork quilt covering it, the one her father had said his mother had made, a grandmother she had never met.

She rose and crossed the landing to the tiny bedroom that had once been hers. Pushing open the door and flipping on the light, she took in furnishings that hadn't changed in a dozen years. The simple twin bed with its knotty pine headboard, the low dresser, the lamp with a checkered shade. Framed photos adorned the walls, images she'd taken the summer Roy had bought her a secondhand 35 mm camera.

She pulled open a dresser drawer to find it full of cards and letters and snapshots. Rifling through them, she pulled a few out to examine. Then huffed out a surprised breath. They were all from her. Her father must have kept everything she'd ever sent him. Only recently had her understanding of his PTSD given her some insight into why their relationship had been so limited. He'd appeared to enjoy having her visit him during the summers, but he'd refused invitations to attend her high school and college graduations, and he'd sent cards sporadically on her birthdays.

Heart heavy, wishing things had been different between them, she opened other drawers. She recognized the sweaters and sweatshirts from when she'd been a teenager. The closet revealed a windbreaker and a rain jacket, apparel more appropriate for the summers she spent with her father in the Sierras than the current snowy autumn. On the top shelf sat a couple of board games and the chess set that had occupied her and her dad over many quiet evenings.

She sniffled, wiping her eyes with her sleeve, and took a deep breath, holding it before letting it out slowly through pursed lips. Despite his limited role in her life, her father had loved her, and that made what she had done to ease his last year worth the price she continued to pay.

Meg descended the stairs to find Declan sitting at the table, laptop open in front of him. Just because he was a cop didn't mean she had to tell him anything. He ignored her, continuing to tap away on the keyboard, and, resigned to the fact that neither one of them was leaving any time soon, she curled up on the sofa, legs drawn under her.

Staring into the fire, she pondered her course of action.

She wanted to use her laptop, and figured Declan had set up a router with WiFi. If she used it to continue the disbursement, however, the transactions could be traced to his IP address. For herself, it didn't matter, because before any of Julius's worker bees had time to trace her location, she'd turn herself in to the police. But she didn't want her actions to expose Declan to danger. There was a chance, though, that he'd already taken steps to hide his IP address. Cops were cagey like that.

"Question."

He paused, fingers poised over the keyboard. "What?" The clipped tone sounded distracted.

"Have you concealed your IP address?"

The look he gave her held all sorts of loaded questions, but all he said was, "Yes."

"Would you mind giving me your WiFi password?"

He rattled off a series of letters and numbers and had Meg scrambling to grab a pen from her bag and write them on her hand. Declan had already resumed typing, a frown pulling down his eyebrows. That was all right with her. She didn't want chitchat, and now she had a task to do that, if she managed it, would make some people ecstatically happy, and one man supremely angry.

Chapter Five

Dex closed the lid on his laptop and pushed back from the table, finally paying attention to the hollow feeling in his stomach. A glance at the clock told him the day had slipped well into the afternoon. He was a bit surprised he'd been able to push Meg to the periphery of his mind, still there but not demanding of his attention, and immerse himself in his writing. A secondary character had been nudging at him, not letting him rest until he gave the little shit a larger part in the story. The guy was a low-life scumbag, but Dex realized now that the character was pivotal to Dex's crime-fighting duo solving the case. He hadn't intended to make the cops romantically involved, but they had also nudged at him until he wrote it that way and it worked.

He eyed his houseguest. She was as absorbed in her work as he'd been in his own. Now that he knew what to look for, he found some resemblance to Roy Evans. The set of her eyes, the winged brows. If he'd known Roy had died, he would have gone to the funeral, given him that last tribute. He wondered how meeting Meg under different circumstances would have turned out.

He wasn't much on dating, didn't have the patience for it, and he absolutely wasn't looking for a relationship, but he knew damn well she intrigued him enough that he would have asked her out. Her current situation probably precluded starting anything. They were at odds over the cabin, and she was in trouble of some kind. He didn't know much about the rules for hooking up, but he had to figure a vulnerable woman was off limits.

Instinctively, Dex had held back the information that his relationship with Roy had been more complex than Dex had claimed. He probably needed to get past his reluctance to be open with people. God knew that fault probably came in at number one on his ex-wife's long list of complaints about him. He'd learned early on that what he shared with his ex she stored up in some vault in her head to be used against him later.

Beyond the personal connection to Roy, the current FBI operation he'd agreed to take part in necessitated keeping quiet. If successful, a particularly nasty character from Dex's past would be spending a good chunk of his life in prison. The upshot was he'd held back, including the fact that LAPD Captain Roy Evans had been Dex's first commanding officer when he'd been a rookie, and had become a mentor throughout his career in law enforcement.

They needed to resolve the cabin issue. Roy had let him use the cabin, but now he was dead. Not that Dex wanted to spend time looking for another place, but he'd do it if he had to. Piled on top of the housing mess was the trouble Meg was in. Not his trouble, but it didn't sit right to let Roy's daughter take off when she was clearly in danger. His obligation to Roy meant he'd figure out the situation, deal with whoever might be after her, then he'd be free to let her be.

He pulled leftover stew from the fridge, scooped some into a bowl, then hit the button to nuke it in the microwave. "You want some of this?"

Her eyebrows were furrowed in a frown, and there'd be nothing left of her thumbnail if she didn't ease up on chewing it. That he'd said something finally registered, because she gave him a startled glance. "What?"

"Stew. That's what's on the menu for lunch. And dinner, for that matter. You want?"

The indecision on her face told him she was debating pulling out another one of those bar things that looked like shredded tree bark, but then she nodded. With BC cradled in her arms, she rose to pad into the kitchen, rainbow-striped socks on her feet.

In height, she came up about level with his shoulder, and while most women her age wore their hair long, the short black curls framing her face worked. But it was the big eyes of the deepest blue under those winged brows that grabbed his attention, and gave him ideas he'd be better off ignoring. The color in her cheeks deepened and he realized he was staring.

"Sure, thanks. Umm, I could make dinner if you like. Repay you for feeding me."

"Yes."

She gave a short laugh. "You're not going to ask me what I'll make, or even if I can cook?"

"I figure you wouldn't offer if you couldn't cook, and I know what's in my fridge. There's nothing weird you could come up with. I'm damned tired of my own cooking so anything you make will be fine."

He pulled his bowl out of the microwave while she transferred stew to a bowl for herself. At the table, he opened the news app on his iPad and scrolled through articles, but instead of immersing himself in current events, he found himself uncomfortably aware of Meg's movements. Despite the timer on the microwave chiming, she stood motionless at the window watching the snow fall. He'd thought of firing up Roy's snowblower but had decided against it. At the moment, it served his purposes to have her snowbound with him in the cabin. He figured once the road was clear she intended to bolt, and he wanted to know what was going on with her before she did that.

Telling himself he was doing this for Roy didn't ring entirely true.

***

Meg set her laptop on the coffee table and stretched her legs in front of her. Declan had put on a heavy coat some minutes before and disappeared out the front door, so she was alone in the cabin. A quick internal survey told her she was on the mend. Despite tiring easily, the achy muscles and headache were better. She'd been able to focus on her computer work, and now a good chunk more of the money was placed where it would do the most good. That it meant she was closer to living in a six by eight concrete box with metal bars didn't bear thinking about. The comfort of a crackling fireplace and the convenience of a laptop with WiFi access would disappear along with her freedom when a judge sentenced her. Upside, maybe the experience of prison would provide depth for her writing.

For now, she'd focus on the positive. Trusting Declan's IP address was untraceable, she sent an email to her mother letting her know she was safe, then gave in to the compulsion and accessed Google. Search results for Julius Merritt yielded no postings dated in the past week, which both surprised and relieved her. The internet would have blown up if the biotech genius had been found dead from a mixture of antianxiety medication and alcohol. Which meant that Julius was alive and would most certainly come hunting for her. But at least adding a murder charge to her other crimes looked less likely.

That there had been no other news made her wary. Julius was all about social media, believing he had to constantly promote his brand if he was going to market his products both nationally and internationally. But Twitter, Instagram, Facebook, even the Chinese WeChat, had all been silent.

She shut down the laptop as heavy footsteps sounded on the porch. Declan swung open the door, filling its frame and bringing the piney smell of the outdoors into the cabin.

"You have a coat?"

"There's my old jacket in the upstairs closet. Why?"

"Snow has stopped. Get the jacket and come out. Wear your boots."

The door slammed as he went out again, leaving Meg staring after him. Deciding to take the words as an invitation rather than a direct order, she retrieved the jacket, pulling it on over her sweatshirt and jamming her beanie on her head before following Declan out the front door.

The cold made her lungs ache when she drew in a deep breath, letting it out to form puffs of vapor in the crisp air. Declan stood on the porch, metal-framed things in his hand.

"What are those?"

He held one up for her to see. "Snowshoes."

"Really? I thought snowshoes were made out of bent wood and rawhide or something equally back-to-nature. These look like they could have been used for a moon walk."

His dark gaze slid over her and she thought maybe she could detect a trace of humor in his almost smile. Shocker.

"Bent wood snowshoes would work fine, but I don't know if anyone from this century makes them like that." He nodded toward the outbuilding. "Your dad had these in the shed, along with a snowmobile and a snowblower." He placed the shoes on the porch floor.

"What are we doing?"

"Going for a walk." He motioned her to step into the molded shoe-shaped piece in the middle of the frame. "You up for it?"

"I think so. But you being nice doesn't change anything, you know. You're in my cabin, and you're a cop. Two reasons we can't be buddies."

"Ex-cop. And I sure as hell don't want to be your buddy."

"Fine. Good. Me either."

"Look, I need to get out of the cabin, get a little exercise." He shrugged. "Thought you'd want to get out, too."

The offer was too tempting, so she nodded in agreement. He knelt in front of her and she stepped into the molded piece. It was designed for someone who wore a much larger shoe size, but Declan cinched down on the straps on first one snowshoe, then the other. She grasped his shoulder for balance, letting go when he rose to his feet.

"You're not taking me out in the woods to murder me, are you?"

"There's a thought."

"Ha, ha." She took an awkward step and grabbed his arm for balance. "Is there a trick to walking in these things?"

She shuffled to the porch steps as he strapped on his own snowshoes. "I'm not an expert. But by trial and error I've learned you keep your stance a little wide to keep one shoe from overstepping the other." He picked up what Meg thought were ski poles. "Go down hills sideways," he continued, "and use these."

He handed her a set of poles.

"Got it. I think."

He used the sideways maneuver to go down the steps, then caught her hand in a warm grasp when she tottered trying to do the same. He released her at the bottom. "Don't you have gloves?"

She shook her head. "I wasn't expecting a snowstorm when I set out."

He pulled a large pair out of a back pocket. "Here, wear these."

She shook her head. "Nope. I'm fine."

She wondered if he was one of those old-fashioned men who thought the job of the adult male was to protect and take care of their women folk. As the daughter of a single mom, she knew women had to protect and take care of themselves. If she hadn't thought to bring her own gloves it meant she would do without, and certainly not rely on a man to provide them for her.

Without comment, Declan pulled on the gloves and set out across the fresh snow, leading around to the back of the cabin. The snowfall had stopped and the clouds looked lighter, making Meg wonder if the storm was done. She trudged after the long-legged man, finding it easier to follow in the path he made, despite his long stride, rather than blaze her own trail. He ascended the slope behind the cabin at an angle, kicking the front end of his snowshoes into the snow to make a series of steps to gain in elevation.

Pretty soon she was huffing, leaning on the poles so much she was sure an octogenarian would have better form. Declan paused about thirty feet ahead of her. She wondered if the beard helped keep his face warm.

"You didn't tell me doing this is like running a marathon."

"It's not that bad. Unless you're not acclimated to the altitude and are recovering from a virus."

Sure, now he was making excuses for her. She hated being a wimp. She pressed on until she stood next to him, leaning on a pole again and panting, the sharp air filling her lungs with what she was sure were ice crystals. Ice crystals in the lungs probably meant pneumonia in her future.

He stood gazing around them as she caught her breath. When she was able to listen beyond her own breathing, she noticed the incredible silence. "Wow," she said in a hushed voice. "It's so quiet."

"Snow muffles a lot of sound. You can barely hear the creek." His voice was quiet, too, and she wondered if the beauty of the setting was having the same effect on him that it was having on her.

Listening hard, she discerned a faint gurgling. A slight breeze picked up, causing a faint whooshing sound through the treetops. "Yeah. It feels like I'm in church."

His intense gaze met hers in complete understanding, making her heart skip a beat. "Exactly. Best church around."

The idea that she and Declan could be on the same frequency, share the same connection to the natural world, was more than a little disconcerting.

Following him up the slope, she realized he favored his right leg. Maybe he'd been injured in the line of duty. What if he'd been hurt and been forced to retire? Would that make him bitter and withdrawn? Curiosity made her a good writer, but sometimes also made her too nosy, an attribute she was sure her reluctant host would resent.

They reached an area where she remembered a trail snaked around the mountain. With the snow covering everything, it was more of a route clear of trees than an actual trail. Declan went that way, giving her an inkling of where they were going. A quarter mile of what she considered grueling mountain climbing later proved her right. They crested the slope and the view slammed into her, breathtaking and awe-inspiring.

She and her father had hiked this trail, and she remembered the incredible vistas of the backcountry—hard granite peaks and the shimmering jewels of mountain lakes reflecting the deep blue of summer skies. The storm that had ushered in an early winter had transformed the scene into a monochromatic landscape, breathtaking in its starkness. Gray clouds obscured the white-capped peaks of the Sierras, and snow frosted the forest of dark pines. The silvery trunks of aspens stood naked of their leaves. To the north, smoke curled into the sky, an indication of cabins tucked into the woods.

"This is so beautiful." Narrowing her eyes, she studied dark gray patches glistening between gaps in the trees. "Are the lakes frozen?"

"Maybe some at the higher elevations. This storm wasn't cold for long enough to get them to freeze their entire surfaces, but maybe along their perimeters."

While they'd been moving she'd been warm, but now the cold was beginning to seep through her jacket. She rubbed her hands together, and Declan said, "Let's get back before you freeze."

They descended the hill using the side-stepping method in the steeper sections. As they neared the cabin, the drone of a powerful engine sounded in the distance. "What's that?"

"Snow plow. They'll probably do the main highway up from town today, and get the lesser roads tomorrow."

Now that she'd learned that her father had given permission for Declan to stay at the cabin, she couldn't see going to the police to evict him. Kicking him out after her dad had said he could stay didn't seem right.

They reached the cabin, and while she'd enjoyed her trek across the fresh snow immensely, her cheeks burned with cold and a pervasive weariness told her she wasn't completely recovered from the flu. She managed to undo the straps of the snowshoes with frozen fingers. Declan held open the door and she entered the warmth of the cabin.

"Oh my God, that feels good."

She shed her jacket while Declan laid a couple more logs on the grate in the fireplace. She held her fingers toward the flames, then pulled them back when the heat brought stabbing pain.

"Here." He pulled off his gloves, then grabbed her hands and held them between his. "Warm them slowly."

Holy cow. Standing so close and with her hands wrapped in Declan's had heat infusing parts of her body from low in her belly to her flushed face. He dispelled the cold better than any fire. *Not good.* She didn't want heat or fluttery feelings or anything resembling attraction where Declan Michael Murphy was concerned. She raised her head to find that dark gaze on her, a speculative look in his expression.

"We having a moment here, Meghan?"

He was nothing if not direct. "No, no moment. Just warming up. And only my dad called me Meghan."

Those lips, the only soft part of his face, ghosted a smile. "That makes one more reason Meghan appeals to me."

Thud. Damn, there went her heart, tripping again.

"Are you flirting with me?" she demanded. "Because that feels like flirting. If you are, then stop. No flirting allowed."

"Right." He let go of her hands and took a step back. Arms crossed over his chest, his expression returned to serious. "We need to talk."

"When my mom started a conversation like that, it meant I was in trouble."

"Are you in trouble?"

"Maybe, but nothing that involves you." She glanced around the cabin. "I probably won't be here more than another day or so. Maybe we can coexist until I'm gone. I'd like to move my stuff up to the little bedroom."

"That's fine. Where are you planning to go when you leave here?"

Jail. But he didn't need to know that.

She shrugged. "There's someone after me, you guessed that right. But I'll go to the police chief you mentioned before that someone can find me."

"Husband? Boyfriend?"

"No, and no. I'm not married, and he wasn't my boyfriend. It doesn't matter. I think he's done some bad things that hurt people, but I'm trying to fix that."

"Why is it on you to fix it?"

"Is this how you conducted interrogations?" When he didn't answer, she sighed, then continued. "It's up to me because I'm the only one who knows what Julius has been doing, and is willing to put a stop to it. Which is why he'll come after me. His world will crumble when what I know gets out."

"Which puts you in danger."

"Yes." She didn't try to soften her response. "If he catches me, he'll try to stop me. But once I go to the police, they'll have to arrest me. I figure I'll be safe if I'm in jail."

"Jesus Christ. What did you do?"

Meg sat on the couch, patting her lap to encourage Buttercup to jump up.

"That cat will make you her slave if you let her."

"Since I don't think they allow jail inmates to have pets, I'll enjoy her while I can." She scratched the cat behind her ears. "That sounds pitiful, doesn't it?"

He sat in the green chair, hands on his knees. "Let me help you."

"Why would you want to?"

After a moment's hesitation, he said, "Roy saved my dad's life. I wouldn't be here if it wasn't for him, so let's just say I'm repaying a debt."

She leaned back against the cushions on the couch. "It doesn't matter. There's nothing you can do. I committed a crime and my debt is to society—to pay it I'll have to go to jail."

"Then it won't hurt for you to tell me what the trouble is."

Tugging on a loose thread on her sweatshirt, she considered his statement. "You're a cop." She held up a finger when he opened his mouth. "Yeah, yeah. I know, *ex*-cop. Doesn't matter. You are who you are, and cops want to solve problems for people."

"Cut the bullshit, Meghan. Tell me why you're on the run, and why you think you'll end up in jail."

The intelligence in those dark eyes, the steadiness she'd detected under the gruff demeanor, made her aware he possessed a solid integrity that undermined her resistance. Add her assessment of his character to the calm levelheadedness he projected, and her deepest and darkest secrets were ready to spill off her tongue. She wouldn't go that far, but she tugged on the chain around her neck, pulling the small black flash drive from under her shirt. "I stole files. They're on this flash drive."

"That's it? You stole some files?"

"They might also get me for attempted murder, but I'm not positive about that."

Chapter Six

"Attempted murder? Give me a break. You wouldn't try to kill anyone."

Meg was already shaking her head. "A lot you know. This was premeditated. I drugged him. I crushed Diazepam and put it in his beer, gave him chips and salsa with extra jalapeños so he'd drink more, and when he passed out, I escaped. I was worried I might have killed him, but since there's been nothing on the internet about his death, I think it will only be attempted murder. Oh, I also embezzled money. A lot of money."

"One thing at a time. Who, Meghan? Who did you drug?"

"If I tell you that, you'll start investigating, or you'll tell your police chief friend and he'll investigate. Not only am I not ready for that, any inquiries from here will be like a giant arrow pointing to this cabin. Which puts you in danger, as well as me."

"I can take care of myself." That dark gaze drilled into hers. "Trust me. You said you escaped, which means you were being held against your will. Is that accurate?"

"By all means, let's be accurate." Meg gave in to the urge to rub the heel of her hand across her forehead where the headache was making a comeback. Stress and worry were her own special recipe for a tension headache. "Sorry. That was uncalled for."

The truth was, Declan disturbed her on several different levels, and she was having a hard time getting past that. Being attracted to him wasn't going to get her anywhere.

Face deadly serious, Declan's gaze remained intense and focused. Stomping down on the flutter around her heart wasn't doing much good.

"He succeeded in manipulating me enough that I wasn't sure what he would do if he knew I was leaving. It's hard to explain," she muttered. There was no way he could understand the control Julius had managed to exert over her.

"Who was he?"

She sighed a deep, heartfelt sigh. She didn't know why she was hesitating. The thing was, as much as Julius scared her, Declan Murphy appeared more than capable of handling him. The temptation to share her burden, if only for a little while, was suddenly too much to resist.

"Have you heard of Julius Merritt?"

A sharp look of heightened awareness passed over his face that she found difficult to interpret. He leaned back in his seat and the rigidity of his pose made her think he was having to force himself to relax. "Entrepreneur. Narcissist. Publicity hound. You drugged that Julius Merritt?"

"Yeah, I guess I did."

"Nothing halfway about you, is there, Meghan?"

"Can't you call me Meg? It's one syllable, much easier."

He shook his head. "No."

Now why should that make her heart do the flippity-flop thing?

"If I have my facts straight, Julius Merritt made his first million with a medical device he designed when he was in college. And now his company has a new product that will supposedly revolutionize treatment for heart disease, and may minimize the need for bypass surgery." Even his gravelly voice affected her heart rate.

"I guess you do know who he is," she stated.

"You could say that."

She waited, thinking he was going to add something else. When he didn't, she continued. "Most people know about his devices for the brain. There's one that helps with the recovery from strokes, and another is supposed to prevent seizures. Not many know about the heart appliance."

"There was an *LA Times* article a month or so ago about the heart thing. They called the device revolutionary, but weren't too flattering about Merritt."

"Yeah. Julius was furious about that part. He wanted to sue the writer."

"Freedom of press."

"That's what his lawyer told him."

"The money you say you stole, it was his?"

"Kind of."

He waited a beat. "Give me the rest, Meghan. It would have to be something damn big to make you steal. You don't even want to eat my food when it's offered to you."

She sighed. He was insightful, she'd give him that. She looked into the fire, knowing it would be easier than watching the condemnation come, as she knew it would. "Julius Merritt advertised a job that could have been written for me. He wanted someone to co-write his autobiography. If hired, I would live in his huge beautiful house in Santa Cruz with its amazing view of the Pacific. I'd have my own suite of rooms in a separate wing to give me privacy, but I'd be available whenever he wanted to work on the book. He also wanted someone who could organize files for his business, and who was also presentable enough to accompany him to social engagements. Kind of like a girl Friday. Basically, I would be at his beck and call, but the job paid enough to make it worth my while. It seemed perfect."

"You were a ghost writer?"

"No, co-writer. We agreed I would get front-cover credit."

"You're a successful writer on your own. Why would you need to take that job?"

"You know I'm a writer?"

"I did a search, found your website. Your latest book has over two hundred Amazon reviews. You have an agent and a publisher. Why did you need Merritt?"

Of course, he'd searched her on the internet. He was a cop. "I'm still getting started as a writer, and not making that much money. I needed more than I was earning with my books." She shifted in her seat, and he narrowed his eyes.

"And the place where your dad was living is top-notch, not a run-of-the-mill VA facility. Which means it was expensive."

It figured that he would put two and two together. "Yes. It was expensive, but worth it to me. I wanted a place where Dad could be happy. Or, if not happy, at least not miserable. The facility I found has a good reputation, and the staff-to-patient ratio is where it should be. They have these incredible gardens where residents can take walks or sit in the sun and they have a view of Monterey Bay. Plus, big bonus, it's in Santa Cruz where I could visit often. Huge, humongous drawback?" She shrugged. "It was damned expensive."

"You took the job to pay for Roy's care."

"Yes. And because part of my compensation was living at Julius's super-gorgeous home overlooking the ocean, I was able to give up my apartment. I had to put my stuff in storage, but I wouldn't have to pay rent. If his book sold well, I would also earn a percentage of the royalties. And I could work on my own writing during my downtime. Being offered the job was like a dream come true."

"What happened to the dream?"

"Cliché time—it turned into a scary nightmare. Julius gave me access to everything, to all his computer files, bank records, everything. In retrospect, it seems stupid on his part, but I believe that in his mind, he's never done anything wrong. He never accepts blame for anything. Any issues with his product, or problems with backers, can be explained away. They are always someone else's fault. It can't be his fault because he's perfect." She paused, remembering how she'd felt when she finally fully understood Julius Merritt's true nature. Realization had come gradually with the accumulation of so many odd inconsistencies in his behavior.

"You get to know someone pretty well when you're writing their biography. The theme running through his life, as he sees it, is that he is a golden child. That God loves him a little bit better than everyone else, and that he has been handpicked for greatness. In effect, he is fulfilling his destiny."

"Sounds like an asshole." Declan's dry tone made her smile.

"Agreed. That realization came in retrospect, because he is also exceptionally charming. He's charismatic, and a lot of people look up to him. He can be generous when it suits him. Those qualities overlay this enormous ego he hides well enough that you don't notice it at first. What you do notice is that he has an explosive personality, which I think is indicative of some sort of mental instability. One second everything's fine in his world, and then something happens that challenges that balance and he blows up, screaming and yelling and throwing things like a toddler."

"You get involved with him romantically?"

"No." One glance told her Declan's intense focus hadn't wavered. "I'm not sure where his sexual interests lie, or if he even has any. He didn't appear to be involved with anyone, and we weren't including any relationships in the biography."

"Why did you continue working for him?"

"It was classic abuser behavior on his part, and I'm angry with myself for not seeing it for what it was sooner.

"Living in his house isolated me, and he didn't like me to have my friends or my mom over. We worked well enough together, though. The book was coming along, and I was getting a handle on the business end of things. I attended several social functions with him."

She rubbed a finger across her thumbnail and clamped down on the desire to chew it. "But he started getting more and more critical. He gave me money to buy better clothes, to go to the 'right' salon for my hair and face. If I was to accompany him, I had to project the appropriate image for the business.

"The first time I witnessed him blow up, his rant was directed at this young guy he'd recently hired for something tech related. It was horrible to watch, appalling really. But after he'd had his tantrum, he apologized, made this grand gesture to placate the guy. He bought him a top-of-the-line computer. But it was more like Julius knew he had to do something to smooth things over, and not because he thought his behavior was wrong."

"He did the same to you." It wasn't a question.

"Eventually, yes. I look back and I see that he started on a small scale to see how I'd react, then ramped up. I feel like an idiot now that I can see how he manipulated me into playing a part. He'd get angry, blow up, do something physically destructive like smash dishes or break a window. And I would soothe him, stroke his ego."

She paused, rubbing the back of her neck to ease the tension. "I knew I had to leave, but I'd gotten into his files enough that I was starting to suspect there was something funny going on with the research results on his medical devices. I wanted time to look at those files when Julius wasn't around."

She shrugged. "Maybe he was starting to suspect something because he began keeping me close to him. When I finally did get a chance to examine the files, I discovered the trials had not gone well, and those findings weren't matched by the claims Julius was making to investors." She sighed. "I was scared he'd catch me, but I didn't want him marketing devices that were harming people. I planned to stay long enough to gather enough information that I had something credible to take to the police."

Declan drummed his fingers on his knee. "Let me get this straight. Merritt was unstable to the point of escalating into rages and destroying property, you realized he was involved in something criminal, but you stayed with him anyway? You put yourself in danger, Meghan."

"Once I recognized his behavior, I thought I could walk the line until I was ready to leave. I was being careful. He was so volatile I was afraid to do anything to set him off, but I gambled that I could manage him until I had the information I wanted. I guess I wanted to leave on my own terms."

"Jesus. He put that bruise on your forehead, so it doesn't look like your plan worked out too well." The exasperation in his voice put her back up, even though he was right.

"I guess not. But that evening, I slipped him the Diazepam and got away." The memory came rolling back like black shadows growing to cover the light. "I don't want to talk about this anymore," she said abruptly, rising to her feet. "I should get dinner started." He didn't stop her, and he didn't say anything else, but he watched her.

Cooking calmed her. There was something soothing in the process of pulling disparate ingredients together and creating something visually appealing as well as satisfying to the appetite.

An examination of the cupboards and refrigerator revealed that Declan cooked, and cooked well, even with the limited conveniences of the small kitchen. She searched through the vegetable bin in the refrigerator, examined the labels of cans in the cupboard, silently cheered when she found yeast packets, then lucked out when she uncovered a couple of mild Italian sausages in the freezer. The hunk of mozzarella in the deli drawer of the refrigerator decided her.

Declan resumed his position at the dining table, laptop open as he tapped away. She'd seen so many guys using the hunt and peck method, but not Declan Murphy. He was all ten fingers on the keyboard. She was pretty sure he was poking around on the internet, finding what he could about Julius Merritt. She couldn't blame him and figured she would be doing the same thing if the situation were reversed.

She mixed flour, yeast, water, olive oil, added a little sugar, and wished for the stand mixer Julius's kitchen had boasted. With the oven at the lowest setting, she put the ball of dough inside to rise and got to work on the toppings. With the microwave on the defrost setting, she thawed the sausages, then removed the casings to crumble and brown the meat in a cast-iron skillet. Chopped onions, mushrooms, and peppers went in the pan next, filling the air with a delectable aroma.

Without a surface large enough to roll out the dough, she decided stretching and pressing it directly into the single rectangular baking tray would work. Half the dough went into the fridge for another day, the rest she worked thin enough for a flatbread pizza. With her hands covered in flour, she tried to push up her sleeves without making a mess.

"Pizza?" The deep voice at her back made her jump. "You're making pizza? Hot damn."

Acutely aware of his nearness, she nodded. "Sans sauce, because there wasn't anything to make it from. We'll have to settle for a garlic butter spread."

"Sounds good to me."

The kitchen was small to begin with, and Declan's large presence made it even more crowded.

"Here." He reached out to tug one sleeve, then the other over her elbows to keep them out of the flour. That small, ordinary act set her temperature skyrocketing. Did his fingers rub against the inside of her wrist on purpose? Or maybe that was wishful thinking on her part. He certainly seemed to be standing close, close enough for her to catch a woodsy scent. It wasn't cologne, but he smelled nice.

Determined to ignore the uncomfortable attraction in hopes it would go away, she moved to the counter to begin assembling the flatbread pizza.

Declan rolled up his sleeves and cleared the sink. Steam rose as he ran hot water into a basin, added a squirt of dish soap that filled the air with the scent of green apples, and started working his way through the dishes and utensils she'd used for prep. With the oven at a higher temperature, she sprinkled cheese evenly over the dough, added the other toppings, ending with a light layer of finely shredded parmesan before sliding the tray into the oven.

While executing the entire process she was hyperaware of the sinewy, corded muscles flexing in Declan's forearms, the long fingers holding dishes and utensils under running water, and his uber-wide shoulders bunching under the red and black flannel shirt.

Rolling her eyes at her lack of mental self-control, she picked up a dishtowel to dry the dishes in the drainer.

The low rumble of his voice broke the quiet. "Merritt has been off social media for the past week. That appears unusual for him."

She wiped a bowl and set it on a shelf. "I already looked for any notifications about his death in the online version of the local Santa Cruz newspaper and elsewhere on the internet and haven't found anything. I'd think if I'd killed him the investigation would get a huge amount of press coverage."

He rinsed the cast-iron pan and dried it, then added a dot of olive oil and smeared it around the bottom before setting it on the stove. He dumped the soapy water and turned the bin on its side. When he dried his hands and leaned back against the counter, that dark gaze settled on her, and she was a bit relieved he'd started talking about Julius, otherwise she might give in to the urge to bite him on the neck.

There was a patch of golden skin between the collar of his shirt and where the dark hair of his beard grew that looked deliciously bitable. Reminding herself that she had at least some self-control, she forced herself not to stare at that spot like a vampire.

"You okay? Your face is flushed."

"Hot oven, you know how it is."

Or hot Declan. Could be either one.

"Right. I accessed what is available to the public on the police and coroner's websites for Santa Cruz, and there are no recorded deaths the day you say you drugged him, or the day after."

She let out a huff of breath. "Okay, that's good."

"Does Merritt know you copied the files?"

Meg tried to figure out why Declan was so interested. Maybe it was simply the cop in him working out a puzzle. Since he didn't seem to be affected by her proximity the way she was by his, she didn't think his attention was personal.

"At first, I didn't think so, but he is smart, and he's tech savvy in specific areas. He relied on others to manage the details of his work, said his job was the big ideas. He staffs an office in Santa Cruz to deal with the business end of his biotech enterprises, and he pretty much trusted the workers there to take care of that side of things so he wouldn't have to."

"What part of the company did you deal with at his house?"

"Whatever had to do with the research side. I was hired to write the biography, but he started asking me to do more work related to the medical devices. His big project right now is launching the heart device in the Asian markets. FDA authorization has stalled, so he's focusing on getting it into China and India. According to him, success there will help support approval here and in Canada. He'd been looking for investors."

"What records did you take?"

She clenched her fingers. "Evidence he was falsifying reports for his heart device. Records showing that during testing there were high levels of catastrophic failure that led to deaths. And evidence that those documents were being altered to indicate satisfactory results."

"Shit."

She nodded. "Exactly. I don't know much about the testing process, but what I do know is that Julius was working with a group of university professors who had formed a research company. Preliminary investigation had shown problems, but Julius refused to believe the reports, and he was going ahead as if the trials had been successful. He had big-time investors on the line and he didn't want to lose them."

"And you have evidence of this on the flash drive that's hanging around your neck."

"I do. I also have the copy of an email from him where he makes the argument that any failures of the devices and subsequent deaths are the blame of the surgeons who implanted them. Deflecting blame is classic Julius Merritt behavior, but it's evidence that he was aware of the deaths related to his device."

"Why didn't you take all that to the police?"

"I did, eventually. At first I wasn't sure what I was finding. Then Dad took a turn. He'd been doing so well, said he liked the assisted-living place. I was able to take him out for breakfast a couple of times a week, we took drives along the coast, hung out in the gardens. He had ischemic heart disease, but he seemed to be holding his own. Until he wasn't. Within a couple weeks doctors were telling me there was nothing more they could do for him and to consider hospice care."

The compassion in Declan's expression echoed her own sadness. She cleared her throat before continuing. "I was dealing with Dad while still trying to do my job. I wasn't paying close enough attention, and later, after the funeral when I was finally able to clear my head a bit, I realized the files indicated *I'd* falsified the records. On top of that, emails had been sent to investors from my account, with the IP source being my laptop. I may be guilty of fraud."

Chapter Seven

"Fuck that. Your computer was hacked. You wouldn't have done anything sketchy like that."

"When Dad died, I was in a fog. It's possible I sent emails out at Julius's direction. But I don't think so. Someone is framing me, and the only person in that house who has the skill to hack into my computer is Julius."

"Bastard."

"Yes." The muscles in her shoulders that had tensed as the story unfolded began to unknot. She hadn't realized how relieved she'd feel to share. And the fact that Declan seemed to believe her had a warm glow encircling her heart.

She continued. "I think Julius was hedging his bets. By making it look like I sent those emails, he was guaranteeing that if the whole thing went sideways, blame would fall on me and he would walk free. It worked brilliantly for him. The emails went to the investors with the false data, and Julius was able to garner over a million dollars of investment money based on that information."

"What did you do once you realized what had happened?"

"When I first discovered that the data had been manipulated, I thought the researchers were at fault, so I told Julius. At the time, he appeared surprisingly cool with it. Given his propensity for temper tantrums, that in and of itself should have been a clue. He said he'd take care of notifying the investors that the records were wrong and offer to return their money. But at the same time he was moving ahead with producing and marketing the devices in Asia. Which meant that patients were receiving heart implants that could likely lead to their deaths.

"It was wrong, and difficult to prove. Once I realized what was happening, I decided to take my chances by going to the police. I figured I could defend myself against charges if I needed to since I absolutely do not possess the skills to falsify scientific test results. Though I guess that might be hard to prove, but Julius definitely has the skills to hack into my computer. So I gathered what information I could and took it to the local police."

"What did they say?"

"That they'd look into it. I never heard anything back from them." Those long weeks waiting to hear from the police had felt like an executioner held a blade over her neck.

"I made a follow-up phone call, got the runaround, and came to the realization that nothing was going to happen. There are some powerful people in that little community who had invested in Julius's company, and they have a lot of influence. I can't be certain, but I suspect a friend of Julius's, or someone he has influence over, may have found out about my accusations and squelched the investigation."

"You could have gone to the FBI."

"Yeah, I probably should have. I might have been more proactive, but I was still grieving over my dad and dealing with the bureaucracy of his death, which I can tell you is no fun. Then I learned that Julius had a meeting with a Chinese businessman named George Liu. Liu is a billionaire with ties to the political elite in China, and Julius had high expectations about how much Liu would invest. I began to suspect that Liu had never been informed that the reports were misleading. Usually, I went to those meetings with Julius, but was told I wouldn't be needed at that one."

"Because Merritt didn't want you tipping his hand."

"Right. I felt like I had to do something, so I emailed Liu and told him about the records. I found the documents showing the true data from the research and sent those as well. I figured I was burning bridges with Julius, but I didn't know what else to do."

The timer on her phone chimed and Meg grabbed at the reprieve. "I need to check the pizza."

Declan beat her to it, pulling the tray out of the hot oven, the mouthwatering aroma filling the air. He set it on the stovetop. "Looks done."

He got cold beers from the fridge, holding up one with a brow raised in question. "You want?"

"What's pizza without beer?"

"Exactly."

Meg slipped the hot pizza out of the pan and onto a cutting board where she used a steak knife to cut it into slices, then carried the loaded board to the table. The stoneware plates Declan set out were the same sand-colored ones her father had used.

Declan opened a bottle and handed it to her. The label showed a noose encircling the words "The Hangman's Lager." She sipped, giving a sigh of appreciation for the rich, yeasty taste. Declan took an enormous bite of pizza, groaning as he chewed. "This is fucking amazing," he said around his mouthful. "You're hired."

She took her own bite and savored the burst of flavors. Swallowing, she agreed, "It is pretty amazing."

They ate in silence for a few minutes until she glanced up and found him regarding her with the thoughtful expression she was beginning to understand meant he was working something out in his head. She didn't want to talk about Julius Merritt or her impending incarceration, so she asked the first question that popped into her head. "What happened to your leg?"

He stopped chewing for a moment, then swallowed and took a pull on his beer without answering.

"Okay, sensitive subject. But I've been spilling my guts, so you should reciprocate."

"Not gonna happen."

She considered that while she worked her way through her slice of pizza. "Okay, your leg's a sensitive subject. Maybe more than your leg was injured. We'll leave that for now." She thought about what she really wanted to know, and decided to go for it. "Are you married? Divorced? Gay?"

"You think I'm gay?"

She shook her head. Nope, no way was he gay. Despite not having acted on them, except for that "moment," as he called it, this evening she was catching sexy vibes, the type that said, "I'd like to get it on with you but it's a bad idea."

"No, not gay. My guess? You're divorced and came up here to heal your broken heart."

He tipped back his bottle again, then wiped moisture from his lip. "Damn. Okay, I am divorced, but I'm not up here to heal a broken heart."

"You must have come up here for a reason, and to get away from your life seems most likely. If it's not because of a still-broken heart, then it's because of your job. Am I right?"

His gaze didn't waver, and she figured if he was trying not to show emotion she was probably on the right track.

"Hmm, that's right, you said you'd quit your cop job. Did you quit because your, you know, parts got injured?"

That got a reaction. "What the hell are you talking about?"

"You didn't want to talk about your injury and I saw you rubbing the upper thigh area, which made me think it was more than your leg that got injured. And guys are so sensitive about their *parts* I thought maybe those had been injured, too. It's nothing to be embarrassed about."

"Jesus Christ, you're a case. Yes, my leg was injured, and no, my *parts* were not injured."

"Well, that's good everything is still intact."

"Eat more pizza, it'll shut you up."

"Not much shuts me up. I'm not one of those introverted writer types."

"More's the pity."

"Are you? The introverted writer type?" When he raised a brow, she gave a gusty sigh. "If you didn't want me to know you're a writer, why leave those craft books stacked up like clues waiting to be discovered?"

He chewed, swallowed, sipped his beer, all while keeping his gaze locked on hers. She was starting to fidget when he said, "I'm working on being a writer, and—" he held up a hand when she opened her mouth to ask another question. "And before you start in on that, I don't want to talk about my writing."

"You make a lot of rules."

"Not rules. Setting boundaries."

"Boundaries are important. Why'd you get divorced, or is that out of bounds, too?"

"I liked you better when you were too sick to talk."

"You're quite the charmer. So the divorce is still a painful subject, and therefore out of bounds?"

He rubbed a hand over his face and down his beard. "Shit. You're not as sweet as you look. Okay, I've been divorced two and a half years. My fault. She's moved on. I've moved on."

"What was your fault, the marriage failing, or wanting the divorce?"

Dark brows lowered. "Do we have to talk about this?"

"Think of me as your therapist. And with me going to jail, you can be pretty sure I won't be around to blab your secrets to anyone."

"You're not going to jail, and I sure as hell don't think of you as my therapist." He took another slice of pizza from the board. "But fine. The marriage failing was my fault."

"Did you have an affair?"

"No."

"Did she?"

"Not really."

"What's that mean, not really? Either she did, or she didn't."

"Not a physical affair."

"An emotional one, then."

"Yeah, I guess. She reconnected with her high school boyfriend on Facebook."

"I'm not seeing how that makes it your fault."

He drummed his fingers, and she could all but see his internal debate as to how much to tell her. "Fine. It was my fault because if I hadn't been working so much, if I'd 'been there' for her, as she'd often complained, she wouldn't have turned to him for something I couldn't give her."

"This time I'm calling bullshit, because that's what it is."

"Is it? And you know so much about it?"

"Maybe I do. What's her name?"

"Meg."

"What, now you're going to call me by my short name?"

"No, I'm not. Her name is Mary Margaret. Mostly she went by Meg."

"Well, crap. That's awkward."

"Not really. You're Meghan."

"Hmm. Regardless, I do know that when you take vows with someone, they better count for something. And an emotional affair is as destructive as a physical one."

"You'll have to tell me about your experience sometime."

"We're not talking about me," she scoffed.

"I like talking about you a hell of a lot better than talking about me."

"Don't say things like that. They make my heart go all flippity-flop and I don't like it."

"Maybe we should try something else to make your heart go all flippity-flop, something more interesting than talking."

She squelched the extra-excited flippity-flop resulting from his suggestion. "Now you're being a jerk."

He leaned back in his chair. "Yeah, I am. Sorry." His tone of voice changed when he urged her to continue. "Finish the story. Merritt must have figured out you contacted the Chinese businessman. I'm guessing his explosive personality manifested itself," his lip curled up, "on the side of your head."

"We're back to me again, are we? Well, okay then. Julius wasn't sure it was me, at least at first. But when Liu told him he'd gotten information that contradicted the research findings, Julius knew it had to come from somewhere in his company, and I was the most likely suspect. But I don't think he was sure, because he didn't confront me directly, at least at first." She spoke softly as the scene replayed out in her mind.

"What did he do?"

She took a sip from her bottle, then set it carefully back on the table. "I was sitting at my desk in my office when I heard him walk through the front door after the meeting with Liu. I was copying the files onto the flash drive and shut down the screen as he came in. You could see the anger barely contained beneath the surface. His being preoccupied was good for me because I know I looked guilty. I knew my role—placate, soothe, stroke his ego. I suggested he go sit out on the patio, that I'd bring him a beer and something to eat to hold him over until I could get dinner cooked."

"You cooked for him?"

"I like cooking." She shrugged. "Anyway, he turned and walked into the front room, picked up a glass bowl valued at more than five thousand dollars, and heaved it into the fireplace. It shattered into a million pieces. What was even more scary was that he wasn't yelling and screaming like he usually did. Containing his emotions isn't typical behavior for Julius. Whatever he was feeling at the moment—happy, sad, frustrated, angry—he pretty much lets everyone know. How can he be soothed and placated if people don't know how he's feeling?"

"That when the fucker gave you the bruise?"

She traced a finger through the condensation on the bottle. She didn't know why she was embarrassed that Julius had hit her, but telling Declan about it was easier when she wasn't looking at him. "He'd never been physically abusive before, and he caught me totally off guard. We were in the kitchen. I was starting dinner and he was leaning against the counter, brooding. Then suddenly he grabbed my arm and swung me around to face him. His face was red, and he had this really ugly expression. He asked if I'd talked to Liu, if I'd sent him those files."

She pushed back her plate and knotted her fingers to keep her hands from shaking. "I denied it. I was scared because I'd never seen him like that. He said Liu knew he was desperate, was acting like his fucking savior, then pulled the rug out from under him, called Julius a con man and said he'd never get money from him. I guess Julius told him he didn't need Chinese money anyway, that he didn't like doing business with liars and cheats."

"Said the liar and cheat."

"The irony didn't occur to him. I was scared because I *had* sent key information to Liu. But I did what I usually did. Tried to calm him, told him he'd get funding from someone else, that Liu would come back, kissing up, begging to get in on the deal. Julius loves it when people grovel." She gave a rueful laugh. "I thought I'd managed it. He loosened his grip on my arm. After that, I'm not exactly sure what happened. I think he jerked me toward him, but I caught my foot on a rug and tripped. Then he hit me. He was lightning fast and it was completely unexpected. The blow snapped my head back and knocked me to the floor."

Declan shoved to his feet, hands balled into fists.

"Next thing I know, he's on his knees beside me, telling me he hadn't meant to hit me, that I kind of stumbled and hit his fist with my head when he tried to catch me. He said I should be more careful."

Declan swung around. "Him hitting you was an accident because you ran into his fist? He's batshit crazy."

"Agreed. I'd already decided to leave. My plan had been to come here because Julius doesn't know about this place, and since the title's still in Dad's name he wouldn't be able to find me. I'd been thinking my next step was talking to the FBI, giving them the files.

68

But I also wanted to buy myself some time because in addition to the files, I'd transferred money from his accounts."

"Why the hell did you do that? You know more than anything else, that's what will make you look guilty."

"I do know that. But Julius was ready to launch his expansion, and if I left that money and the devices became available in Asia, people were going to die. What happened that night made me realize Julius is completely unbalanced, and I had to get out. I didn't feel safe staying with him, especially because I know he keeps a loaded gun in his nightstand."

"Something you have in common."

"Ha. I didn't start carrying my dad's gun until recently."

"Finish it. Tell me the rest."

"Right. It's pretty simple, really. I knew there was unused Diazepam in the medicine cabinet. Julius went out on the deck, and I did a quick online search to find the dose that would knock out a two-hundred-and-forty-pound man, but not kill him. I learned that alcohol magnifies the effects of the drug." She shrugged. "I made salsa with extra jalapeños, chips with extra salt, and crushed the Diazepam to a powder and poured it into his beer. He was out in twenty minutes."

Declan regarded her with a ghost of a smile on his face. "I shouldn't admire that, but damn, you're good."

"Yeah. Pretty scary how easy it was. I gave myself enough time to get to my mother's house before I called for medical assistance. As you can see, any lawyer will have an easy time getting a conviction for attempted murder."

"I don't think they could prove attempted murder. How did you get the money?"

She chewed on her thumbnail, then lowered her hand when she caught him watching her. "I had all his passwords. Can you believe, he never changes them? I accessed one of his accounts and transferred a large amount of money. It's gone now."

"What do you mean it's gone? What did you do with it?"

"Gave it away."

"Explain, Meghan." Not sure why it sounded sexy when he said it, she decided she'd never again complain about his use of her unabbreviated name.

"Have you heard of microgrants?"

"Microloans, yes. I'm guessing the grants don't have to be paid back."

"Right. I gave the money away."

"How much are we talking about?"

"A little under a million dollars."

He gave a low whistle. "Where exactly did the money go?"

"Like I said, I gave it away. To women mostly. Women like my mother who struggled to raise their children without a husband. I gave a grant to a woman in Ethiopia who will use it to dig a well in her village so the girls there won't have to walk three miles every day to get water. I found a woman in Afghanistan whose family shunned her after she was raped and became pregnant. After she finishes her education she will have the funds to start a school for girls where her daughter will attend.

"Then there's the woman in the southside of Chicago who wants to be a doctor and practice medicine in her old neighborhood, the same neighborhood where her brother was shot dead after pointing a BB gun at the police."

"He shouldn't have been pointing a BB gun at police."

"No, he shouldn't. And I'd hate to be a cop in that situation. But neither should the boy be dead."

Declan nodded. "And now the money's gone."

"Yes. I disbursed the last of it earlier today."

He rose to his feet, picking up the board where only a few crumbs remained of the pizza to carry to the kitchen. "You're not going to jail," he said over his shoulder.

She almost believed him.

Chapter Eight

Meg sat up in the dark, fingers clutching the quilt in a death grip, not sure if a bad dream had woken her or a noise from inside the cabin. She'd moved to the little room she'd slept in all those long-ago summers. Through the square windowpane high in the apex of the A-frame, tiny specks of light told her the sky had cleared and stars were glittering from millions of miles away.

The bedroom door swung open silently, the motion barely discernable in the faint glow from a nightlight on the landing. A call for Declan nearly escaped her lips when she felt a weight land on her feet. She let out a wheezy breath when Buttercup climbed over the mounds created by her knees to stand on her stomach.

Meg stroked the cat behind her ears and felt her heart rate level out as the little calico began a gentle purring. She settled back on her pillow, Buttercup a warm and comforting presence curled against her.

The next time she opened her eyes, daylight streamed in through the high window. She lay for a moment, squeezing her eyes against sudden tears. Today was the day.

Pushing against the melancholy, she rose and padded across the small landing to use the upstairs bathroom. She was brushing her teeth when she heard voices. She recognized Declan's deep tones in conversation with another man. She rinsed, then stepped out onto the landing, padding quietly in her stockinged feet.

The conversation came from the porch, then the voices faded as the men moved away. A minute later the door opened, and Declan stepped inside.

***

Dex shut the door. An early morning phone call to his contact at the FBI, plus his conversation with his friend the police chief, had left him irritated. The situation was getting more complicated, and he didn't like complicated.

He glanced up to find the source of that complication at the top of the stairs. Tousled hair, heart-shaped face, eyes big enough to drown in. The slap of attraction wasn't welcome. He'd been doing fine on his own, writing, doing repairs on the cabin. Getting his head around the fact he was no longer a cop, that he'd sucked as a husband. But in the short time since she'd arrived, Meg had burrowed under his skin. Made him *feel* when not feeling was a whole lot easier. Chasing an armed banger through a filth-strewn alley in LA was preferable in every way to having his heart beaten to a pulp one more time.

But protective instincts were hard to bury, and the urge to protect her from the fucker Julius Merritt was undeniable. In Dex's years on the force he'd worked with plenty of women physically and mentally able to take care of themselves in about every situation, and without doubt Meg was one of them. But for some messed-up reason she compelled him to pull out his metaphorical sword and stand between her and the dragon.

She descended the stairs slowly, her gaze locked on his. He rocked back on his heels, tucking his hands in his back pockets to keep from reaching for her. Thinking about what he'd like to do once he had them on her only ramped up his frustration. Developing a thing for her was damn distracting and inconvenient, and not what he'd been looking for.

"Who was that?"

Low and easy, even her voice was sexy. "Brad Gallagher, police chief of Hangman's Loss."

"Was he looking for me?"

Dex shook his head. "No. And he didn't mention the car out front, or the small-sized boots by the door." He shrugged. "Probably thinks I got lucky."

"A lot he knows."

"Yeah. Anyway, snowplow came through about an hour ago. I already cleared the driveway. Get yourself some breakfast and we'll head into town."

"To see him?"

The bleakness in her expression had him beating back the dragon-slayer urge once again. "Not you, me. I helped Brad with a case involving his sister a while back. It's getting close to the court date and I'll need to testify. Brad was in the area and dropped by to tell me the lawyers are in town today taking depositions. Getting mine done in Hangman's Loss saves me from having to drive to the county seat in Bridgeport."

She stood straighter, shoulders squared, as if bracing for a blow. "Then this is it. I'll go with you and turn over the flash drive to your police chief friend." Knuckles gripping the bannister showed white. "I'll tell him everything. I won't try to get bail because I'll be safer in jail where Julius can't get to me."

"You're not going to jail."

"You keep saying that, but once I tell the chief I slipped drugs into Julius's beer and embezzled that money, he won't have any choice."

Dex was working on that, but couldn't say anything. She pulled at him, made him *feel* despite the lock he'd put on his emotions. Not able to stop himself, he reached for her hand, easing her grip from the rail and holding it firmly between his. Her startled expression told him he'd surprised her, but he didn't let go.

"Don't talk to him yet." He shook his head when she opened her mouth in protest. "Hang on. First, you're not saying anything to the police without talking to an attorney. There's a lawyer in town who's smart. I called her and she said she has time this morning so you have an appointment in forty minutes. If that doesn't work for you, you can cancel, but I called her on the off chance she'd have time today, and so you'd have the option.

"Second, Brad will be busy giving his own deposition, so he's not going to mind waiting. You're safe right now. Even if Merritt is after you, with that storm we had, the passes will be closed until the plows can get through, so the only way over the mountain today is by air, and the closest airport that's not snowed in is probably Reno. If he's not already here, he won't be getting to Hangman's Loss today." And idiot that he was, Dex wanted a little more normal with Meghan Bennett before diving into the battle to keep her out of jail.

Her shoulders visibly relaxed. "Okay," she uttered the word on a gusty breath. "I'll wait until tomorrow to talk to the chief. But I can't pay for an attorney until I can access my bank accounts."

"I'll take care of it."

"Only if you'll let me pay you back." At his nod, she continued, "I can drive my car to the attorney's office, then come back here."

He interlaced his fingers with hers and tugged her closer. He liked the feel of her hand in his a little too much. "Come with me. The sun's out and it's warming up outside. If you finish with the attorney before I'm done giving my statement, you can check out the town, walk around a bit without freezing. We can go out to lunch after."

She hesitated, then must have weighed the options in favor of his plan, because she smiled, twin dimples in her cheeks, and he felt the hit straight to his gut. He was doomed.

The entire package was seductive enough, but he was a sucker for dimples. Going with the impulse, he did what he'd wanted to do since the moment he'd opened the door to find her standing on his doorstep. He dipped his head and pressed his lips to hers. A brief kiss, but firm enough to let her know he was interested.

The sexy little catch in her breathing did nothing to stop the blood arrowing from his brain straight south. She didn't jerk back, and she didn't punch him. Good signs as far as he was concerned. He eased back, loosening his grip on her hands.

She was already shaking her head. "Oh, no, mister. You started it. You're not backing out now."

She reached up to tug the collar of his shirt and brought his head down, going up on her toes to lock her lips on his in a kiss that about knocked him out at the knees. He gripped her hips and pulled her in to get the full-body effect and went with it.

Wild and electric like the summer thunderstorms that whipped through the mountains, the kiss took them deeper than he thought either of them expected. When her lips left his and she dropped onto her heels, he stepped back carefully as if a single false move would set off unstable dynamite.

She cleared her throat. "Wow."

"Yeah." He had to admit it was gratifying to see she wasn't making any attempt to hide that the kiss had knocked her on her ass, figuratively speaking, too. "I had a feeling."

"Did you?" He stifled a groan when she ran her tongue over her lips as if savoring the last trace of him. "Uhm, we shouldn't do that again."

"You think after we've had that taste we won't want the full meal?" He agreed with her. They absolutely should not get tangled up together, but he couldn't seem to shut up.

"Is 'full meal' code for sex?"

He gave a snort of laughter. That she clouded his brain with lust at the same time as making him laugh was an intoxicating combination. "Hell yeah, it's code for sex."

"I thought so." She backed up a full step. "Declan Murphy, you need to stay away from me. I'm going to jail."

"You're not going to jail."

"You don't know that, and regardless, mixing up with you risks my sanity. No more kisses."

"I don't think either of us will be able to stop that from happening."

She shook her head emphatically. "We'll forget this little incident ever occurred." She held up her hands like she was trying to stop traffic, reaching a foot back to climb the stairs backwards and keep a wary eye on him as she retreated.

"Did you make coffee already?"

He shook his head, and she said, "Good, then we'll pick some up in town. That'll get us out of the house quicker. Safer that way. There will be no need for more kisses."

"You know, every time you say 'kiss' my mind goes crazy with all the places I'd like to put my lips on you."

Her cheeks flushed pink and made him want to scoop her up and tumble her into his bed to put the fantasy into practice.

She backed up another step and mimed zipping her lips. "No more mention of kisses. The word 'kiss' is officially out of my vocabulary."

***

Meg sat in the passenger seat of the 4Runner as Declan shifted from second to third on the winding mountain road. Two days before she had been ill, traveling this road toward the cabin, hoping to hole up until she recovered from the flu and could deal with Julius. Now she still had to deal with Julius, jail remained a dark stain on the horizon and getting closer every minute, but with Declan at her side she didn't feel so alone. The reprieve he offered was only temporary, but she savored it nonetheless.

With the skies clear and the sun shining, the melting snow made little rivulets along the road and already pine trees were dumping the heavy clumps from their branches. Declan eased on the brakes, coming to a stop to allow a trio of deer to pick their way across the road on impossibly slender legs.

"Deer. Oh my. They're so beautiful. And there's a baby. How cute." The look he sent her had her tilting her chin. "So? I don't live in the mountains where it's common to see deer. And even if I did I'd still be excited."

"Deer make you excited."

"I love seeing animals in the wild. So yeah, I get super excited when I see deer."

"I don't think you can say that either."

"What, deer?"

"Excited."

"I can't say 'excited'? Why not?"

"Same result as 'kiss.'"

She didn't dare look at his lap for evidence of exactly how the word might be affecting him. "You're easy if a few little words are enough to get your engine going."

He glanced at her, right eyebrow rising in a dark arc, the curve of what she now knew were luscious lips forming a grin. "Never had that problem before. Must be something about you."

"Enough. I'm imposing a moratorium on flirty talk."

He must have realized she was serious because he gave a brief nod. "Okay."

Determined to get the most from her last day of freedom, Meg relaxed in her seat, taking in the scenery. The deep cerulean blue sky contrasted markedly with the gray granite soaring mountain peaks, their slopes in stark white. Living in Santa Cruz on gorgeous Monterey Bay there had been plenty of days so beautiful her heart ached with it, but the Sierras held a different kind of beauty, rugged and untamed. If prison wasn't in her future, she could relocate here. The last thought had her pushing resolutely against the despair gathering like a dark cloud.

They dropped in elevation as they neared town, the 4Runner easily handling the patches of black ice that slicked the stretches of road still shaded from the sun. More cabins were visible through tall trunks, and the pine forest grew thinner. Hangman Lake came into view, a calm serene surface reflecting back the blue sky. A sign for a resort flashed by, and tiny cabins sat nestled among the trees with the lake a picturesque backdrop.

"A friend owns Hangman's Best on Main Street, it's a bakery/café deal. We can get coffee there. The attorney is right around the corner. When you're done, if you want to take a walk and see the town, that's a good place to start." He slowed as they entered Hangman's Loss and the road they were on became Main Street. "Give me your cell number and I'll give you a call when I'm done. We can meet back at the café for lunch."

"I thought you said there was no cell service up here."

He glanced at her. "There's service in town, but it's inconsistent at the cabin. Sometimes you get lucky."

She was already shaking her head. "It doesn't matter, I can't give you my number. My cell is turned off, and I'm using a burner phone only for absolute emergencies. I don't want to make it any easier for Julius to find me."

"He'd have to have the number to trace it."

"I know, but it still makes me nervous."

"That's irrational."

"Probably, but I left it at the cabin, so it's a moot point."

They pulled up at a stop sign, and Declan hitched up his hip to reach into his pocket and pull out his phone. He handed it to her. "Take mine. I'll call from the police station when they're done with me. You can tell me where you are and I'll pick you up."

"You don't have to give me your phone. I'll be fine."

Apparently, there was no arguing with Declan Murphy when he set his mind to something. He parked on the street, and when Meg climbed out of the vehicle, she still held his phone in her hand. An A-frame sign on the wooden boardwalk read "Hangman's Best Café and Bakery." She breathed in deep the crisp mountain air that held the scents of pine and woodsmoke. Declan strode forward to open the door for a woman with a colorful knit cap on her head pushing a double-wide stroller.

The woman paused at the entrance when she spied them. "Dex, it's so good to see you." She reached up to give him a hard hug, a move that seemed to catch him by surprise. She pushed the stroller that looked like it could climb mountain trails all on its own while Declan held open the door. They followed her into the building.

"Brad told me you popped out these guys." He bent down to lift the blanket draped over the stroller.

"'Popped out' makes it sound way too easy, especially since there were two. Mason was over seven pounds, and Keeley slightly under, and let me tell you, they didn't just pop out."

"Aah, okay." Declan's discomfort made Meg smile. "You doing good?"

"Still a bit sore down there." She laughed when he winced. "I'll spare you the details, but yes, I'm doing fine."

Declan motioned Meg forward.

"Maddy, this is Meghan, a friend who's visiting for a few days."

The woman turned her attention to Meg. "Nice to meet you. These two in the stroller are Mason and Keeley."

Meg bent forward to examine the tiny infants bundled against the cold, their cheeks and noses pink, both with eyes the dark blue of newborns. "Oh, they're beautiful. When were they born?"

"Two and a half weeks ago. You'd think they were the first babies on the planet as much as their father dotes on them."

"That's sweet."

The amazing aroma of cinnamon and coffee made Meg's stomach growl. A door to the back swung open, and a shriek from behind the counter was followed by rapid footsteps. A woman with dark blonde hair, a white apron tied around her waist, skirted a display case and rushed forward. She gave Maddy a quick hug, then turned her attention to the babies.

"Oh, they're both awake. Which one can I hold? Don't make me beg."

Maddy gently lifted the baby with the yellow bow on her fair head from her bed in the stroller and handed her to the woman, who was wiggling her fingers.

"Come here, my sweet little love nugget of joy," she crooned. "Your cousin has missed you so much."

"You and Diego were over last night and saw them both, Eva," Maddy stated.

"Yes, and that was a long time ago, wasn't it, darling?" She nuzzled the baby's rosy cheek, then raised her head to smile in Declan's direction.

"Hey, Dex, nice to see you decided to return to civilization."

"Been busy." He laid a hand on Meg's shoulder. "This is Meghan."

"Nice to meet you. If you don't mind, I'm going to take this little girl to the back and show her off."

She disappeared through the swinging door. Maddy turned to Meg, speculation dancing in her eyes. "Meghan, I'm glad you're able to get Dex here out of his cave."

Before Meg could reply, a tinkling bell sounded as the door opened to let in a lean man wearing a dark knit cap and several days' growth of beard. While Meg saw him do a quick scan and was sure his glance took in every person in the restaurant, it zeroed in almost immediately on Maddy. He stepped forward, took her hands in his, and pulled her into a kiss that was steamy enough to melt all the snow clear to the surrounding counties.

Declan coughed loudly and made an exaggerated clearing-of-his-throat sound. The man loosened a hand to hold up his middle finger in Declan's direction with his lips still locked on the woman who was busily kissing him back.

Meg couldn't help but be fascinated by the interactions of the members of the group and the ease with which they included Declan. She'd pegged him as a loner, but it was obvious that despite that tendency, these people counted him as one of their own.

The man loosened his hold and Meg gave a startled gasp when Maddy pulled back a clenched fist like she would sucker punch him. He must have been expecting it because he caught her hand before she could let fly. "What the hell, Blondie?"

"Don't you ever leave me again."

"I was gone two days for training. That's it."

"Two long days. I missed you, and your children missed you."

"I missed you more."

"God, Ross, that's sappy," Declan muttered.

"Got a problem, Murphy?"

Declan ghosted a smile and shook his head. "You two should take it to the back. There are impressionable children present, as well as public decency laws to uphold."

The man's gaze slid from Declan to Meg as he ran his hand down Maddy's arm and interlaced his fingers with hers. Then he bent over the stroller. "Hey, I'm missing a kid."

"Eva has Keeley. Don't pick him up."

Too late. The man Declan called Ross had undone the straps and was lifting the baby from his seat. "He missed his dad. Didn't you, little man?"

"You know he'll want to be nursed now, don't you?"

"Of course he does, how else is he going to grow?"

Maddy tipped her head to rest on the man's shoulder. She angled a look up at him. "I thought you weren't coming home until late this evening."

He brought up her hand with his free one and kissed her knuckles. "I came back early to meet with the lawyers and give my deposition while they're in town."

"Whatever the reason, I'm glad you're home. Logan," Maddy continued, motioning to Meg. "This is Declan's friend, Meghan."

"I prefer Meg. It's nice to meet you all."

Declan addressed the group, "We came in to get coffee, then Meghan has an appointment and I'm heading over to the police station. I'm giving my statement to the lawyers, too."

"I guess we're all being deposed, then," Maddy said. "I'm supposed to go this afternoon. I told them I couldn't be there until after the lunch rush. Mom's coming to pick up the twins and she'll take care of them until I'm done with the lawyers. I'm glad they're getting the process going. The sooner we can get the trial started and that sick bastard Horvath is on his way to prison, a better place the world will be."

Logan kissed the top of Maddy's head. "He'll be behind bars for the rest of his life and never again be able to destroy lives." He must have caught Meg's confused expression because he moved to clap a hand on Declan's shoulder. "Have this guy tell you about it."

More customers came in and set the little bell over the door jingling. Two women with a half-dozen kids between them crowded around the display case. Eva returned Keeley to the stroller and took up her place behind the counter. The moms ordered a couple of giant cinnamon rolls that Eva cut into sections and placed on small plates. Once the small crowd had moved to the dining room, Meg ordered a toasted bagel and coffee.

Sipping her coffee, and with her bagel and cream cheese wrapped in a napkin, she said good-bye to the others and followed Declan out the door.

He walked with her around the corner and pointed to an older Queen-Anne-style home with a sign in the front yard that read "Nguyen and Ricketts, Attorneys at Law." "That's where you want to go. Your appointment is with Brenda Nguyen."

"Okay."

He sipped from his to-go cup, expression thoughtful as she munched on her bagel. "You going to be okay on your own for a couple of hours? If you want, I can give you the keys and get a ride to the police station with Logan. That way you can take the truck back to the cabin if you get bored."

"I won't get bored. I'll be back here at the café in two hours, and I can hang out if it takes you longer. Don't worry about me."

He gave her a thoughtful look, then paused briefly before turning and walking to the 4Runner. As the vehicle roared up the street, Meg wondered at that hesitation. For a second there she was sure he'd had the impulse to give her a good-bye kiss but had thought better of it.

Chapter Nine

Meg finished her bagel and coffee, finding a waste can for her trash before walking to the attorney's office. Less than an hour later, she walked out again. Brenda Nguyen was sharp, and had recommended against admitting to the police that she'd taken money or files from Julius, and even when Meg insisted that she would tell Bradley Gallagher everything that had happened, had still agreed to represent her.

Meg determinedly set aside the worry to enjoy the remainder of her day. She returned to Main Street and set off down the wooden boardwalk under the deep shingled eaves that protected it from the snow, features that accentuated the western feel of the town. Stores had signs hanging from wrought-iron brackets, and red and gold chrysanthemums in large pots added autumn-toned splashes of color. She wondered if shopkeepers dragged the planters in at night or if the fall flowers were hearty enough to survive the cold nighttime temperatures.

She passed an outdoor gear store that boasted a display window filled with the latest hiking and ski equipment. A little farther down she came across a window presenting beautifully woven blankets in hues that reminded her of the local landscape. The hanging sign read "Sisters' Homegrown Treasures" over a design of three interwoven hearts.

Meg stepped inside to find attractive displays featuring local honeys, jams, jellies, and preserves. There was pottery in Southwestern motifs, and burnished silver and polished stone jewelry that the card on the counter explained were made from materials found in the nearby mountains.

"Hello, dear. Are you looking for anything in particular?"

"No, I—"

She broke off when she looked up to find three older women wearing matching turtlenecks of saffron yellow, hair tinted the same exact shade of currant red, and identical expressions of polite inquiry.

"Ah, no, thank you. I'm not buying today. Is it okay to look?" At their synchronized nods, she added, "You ladies make quite an impact."

"We always have. We're triplets, you know," one of the trio said, beaming a smile full of delight. "Though as the firstborn, I'm the eldest."

"That's amazing. You and your sisters have a beautiful store."

The oldest sister seemed to be the spokeswoman. "Thank you. We're pleased you've dropped in. Feel free to wander, and let us know if you need any assistance," she offered.

Meg took her time, enjoying the freedom of having nowhere to be. The triplets had put together an eclectic collection of goods made entirely by craftspeople who lived in the area. She particularly liked a painting of Hangman Lake that caught perfectly the moment at dawn when the sky shimmered between darkness and light, the silhouette of a lone fisherman casting his rod providing a focal point.

She flipped over the tag. A bit pricey, but not impossible. It would look nice in the cabin hanging next to the fireplace. Her thoughts crashed to a halt. She couldn't buy the painting, and she wouldn't be living in the cabin for a long time. She wasn't sure, but had a feeling hanging art in one's jail cell wasn't the done thing.

Determined not to let the knowledge of where her future lay dim the shine on her day, she waved good-bye to the color-coordinated triplets and returned to the boardwalk. A man in dark aviator glasses sat on a wooden bench, phone pressed to his ear. Hard to tell with the mirrored lenses, but the sensation that he was watching her as she window-shopped gave her an itch between the shoulder blades. She stopped in front of an antiques store and looked back over her shoulder. The man had disappeared.

Hangman's Loss was small, and it took no more than an hour to browse the shops from one end of Main Street to the other. While the temperature was in the chilly range, if she kept moving she was warm enough. Leaving the covered boardwalk, she followed signs to climb a hill to the rusty gate of the cemetery. Someone, a caretaker perhaps, had already cleared the paths. Strolling among tombstones aged by time, she wiped snow from some of them, intrigued to discover several that gave snippets of the history of the small town of Hangman's Loss.

The epitaph on one marker from the late 1890s stated that the dearly departed woman had died three days after delivering a stillborn child. Meg wondered if a broken heart had hastened her death.

Then there was the marble gravestone for a young man of twenty-two who had been mortally injured from an explosion in a mine, and another only a year older who had died after being stabbed in a barroom brawl. It seemed that Hangman's Loss had its own Wild West history.

She moved on, reading the epitaphs as she strolled the grounds. The saddest were the tiny markers for infants, some not even named, who had died in the days when being born into the world was a risky business.

Despite the heartache reflected in the dedications to "most loved father" and the "now sleeping angel," walking through the rows of graves brought a kind of peace. It was comforting to know that the people of the town still cared about their ancestors enough to pay for the upkeep and maintenance of the cemetery.

A more contemporary pink granite marker caught her attention. Meg read the inscription that had her heart swelling in her throat. "Lily Patricia Ross, much loved daughter of Madison and Logan." The birth and death dates were far, far too close together. The couple she'd met earlier had lost a baby girl some ten years before. She wondered if Declan knew their story.

From the cemetery she made her way toward the lake. A park encircled the northern tip, a sign proclaiming it Founder's Park. The itch was back, and she scanned back the way she had come, but didn't see anyone. She brushed the snow away from a plaque on a stone monument, then returned her freezing fingers to her pocket.

The plaque told the story of a man accused of a crime he hadn't committed, who had escaped a noose hung by a posse from a tree that still grew in the park, thus providing the name for the lake and the town of Hangman's Loss. In all the times she'd visited her father at the cabin, she hadn't learned as much about the town's history as she had in the past hour.

A creek tumbled from the lake, and Meg followed a path along its course that led back into town. She had turned onto a road she thought would take her to Main Street when the phone in her jacket pocket vibrated. The number was unassigned. She answered, not liking the hesitation in her voice. "Hello?"

"It's me." Declan's low tone sounded in her ear and made her heart trip. Damn, she was in trouble.

"The lawyers deposed me first, so I'm done. Where are you?"

Meg looked around but didn't see a street sign. "I'm not sure, but I think only a block or two from Main Street. I'll be back at the café in a few minutes."

"Do you want me to find you and pick you up?"

"No, I'll meet you there."

"Okay, I need to have a quick word with Brad, then I'll be on my way."

Meg trudged up the road and made the turn onto Main Street. She passed a pizzeria, pausing to look at the menu taped to the inside of the window. A movement in the glass caught her eye. The window reflected the street behind her, and on the opposite boardwalk stood the man with the aviator glasses she'd noticed before. With his glasses pushed to the top of his head, he held his phone in front of him, and it looked like he was taking pictures. Of her. She whipped around, and the man turned and busily began tapping like he was sending a text.

"Hey," she called out.

Aviator Guy shoved the phone in his pocket and began striding quickly up a side street.

She stepped off the boardwalk, intent on following him, and the blare of a car horn had her jumping back, mouthing "sorry" to the alarmed driver. When she looked for him again, the man had vanished.

Not sure whether she was making something of nothing, Meg walked the block to the café. Seeing the man twice on her walk didn't mean he was following her. He could be a tourist who like her was checking out the town. But tourists didn't usually travel alone. And what about him taking pictures? Maybe he liked the western motif and was taking pictures of the buildings, and she happened to be in the shot.

Perhaps, but she couldn't shake the uneasy feeling.

Pushing back on the niggling worry, she looked for the 4Runner among the vehicles parked on the street. Not seeing it, she figured Declan hadn't arrived yet. She stepped into the warmth and delicious smells of the café. The phone vibrated again, and she frowned at the screen. Caller id indicated the incoming call was from "Cassandra." A girlfriend? Family member? What if it was an emergency? After a brief internal debate, she tapped on the screen.

"Hello?"

A long pause, then, "Oh, hi. I had to check to make sure I hadn't called the wrong number, but this is Declan's phone. Who is this?"

"I'm Meghan, a friend of his." She figured using Meghan was wiser than introducing herself as Meg, given the ex-wife business. And saying she was a friend was kind of true. "I'm sorry to answer, but he loaned me his phone."

"Really." She drew the word out into three long, suggestive syllables that had Meg cringing.

"Ah, it's not like you seem to be thinking." At least she didn't think so, though there had been that kiss. That really exceptionally hot kiss.

"It's not like Dex to give his phone to anybody. Are you close friends?"

"No, not really." She hoped to god Cassandra wasn't a girlfriend. Pressing on with the awkward conversation, she asked, "Can I take a message?"

The door gave a jingle and Declan walked into the café.

"Hold on, he's right here." She all but shoved the phone in his hand. "Sorry, but I thought it could be important. It's a woman named Cassandra. I hope I didn't get you in trouble."

Eyes on hers, he put the phone to his ear. "Cass, what's up?" He listened intently, then said, "No, no, and no. That clear enough?" Then a minute later, he said, "I'm hanging up now," and did.

"I'm so sorry. Was that your girlfriend? I don't want to mess things up for you."

"I wouldn't have kissed you if I had a girlfriend. Cassandra's my sister. My nosy sister."

"Oh." His statement did nothing to settle her rapidly beating heart. "You hung up on her."

"Give her a few hours and she'll call back, she always does. Let's order, I'm starving."

They turned to the counter to find Maddy watching them with avid interest. "Hey, you two," she said brightly. "I didn't really mean to listen, but you were right here, and I won't ask, because that would be rude, but if one of you volunteered to tell me whether you're together, you'll be saving me from dying of curiosity."

"That's enough to give me a headache," Declan complained. "Don't you have someone else to torment? Where's Ross? He's a good choice."

Maddy pouted. "He got a call from Brad that they're ready for him to give his deposition. Which is really mean because he got back like a minute ago and I hardly had any time with him. Anyway, back to what I was saying. I was wondering if you two are, you know, friends or 'friends.'" She used her fingers to put air quotes around the last word.

"I thought you weren't going to ask. And didn't I help save your life? You could show your gratitude by minding your own business."

Undaunted, she said, "Spoilsport."

"You bet." He turned to Meg. "You ready to order?"

"Wait a minute. You saved her life? What happened?"

Declan rolled his eyes. "Hungry, remember?"

Maddy beamed at her. "Meg, anytime you want to talk, come on by. I work the lunch hours at least three days a week. You can leave Dex at the cabin and we can have coffee and a nice chat."

"I might just do that." Meg's smile felt forced. Planning to meet a new friend for coffee wasn't likely to be in her future for the next couple of years.

They gave their order, Meg glad that she had enough cash to pay for her meal. Declan offered but hadn't argued when she covered her own. Paying the attorney Brenda Nguyen wouldn't be a problem, because by the time Meg got the bill, she wouldn't be worried about tipping Julius off to her whereabouts and could access her own bank accounts.

She sat across from Declan at a table by the window that gave a charming view of Main Street with the mountains jutting into the sky in the distance. Seeing Declan interacting with his friends showed her a new side of the man, one she found appealing.

A tiny woman wearing a brightly colored embroidered blouse that reminded Meg of Central American art set their meal in front of them, and when Meg gave her thanks, she nodded and left without uttering a word.

Meg bit into her BLT avocado panini and groaned her appreciation of the blending of flavors. Maddy had assured her the rosemary sourdough was baked on premises and was delicious. Declan flashed strong teeth as he bit into his roast beef and cheddar on rye.

After swallowing, Meg shared, "I didn't have much of an impression of Hangman's Loss when I visited my dad. We spent our time hiking and fishing, but we didn't come into town much. But I like the feel of it, at least what I saw today. The people are friendly. Have you ever been in the shop called Sisters' Homegrown Treasures? The women who own it are identical triplets, and have to be over seventy years old."

"The Hensley triplets. Haven't been in the shop, but I've met them. Can't tell them apart."

"They're—" Meg broke off when she spied the guy with the aviator glasses on the boardwalk in front of the store next door to the café. He was taking a picture of the 4Runner's license plate. "Do you see that man? Do you see him?" She pointed out the window.

Declan's head whipped around. Aviator Guy was now opening the driver's door of a nondescript brown sedan.

"That guy with the aviator sunglasses. I saw him a couple times this morning—the second time I thought he was taking pictures of me. And just now he took a picture of your license plate." Even as she spoke, the sedan eased into the light traffic. Declan peered intently through the window, then pulled a pen from his jeans pocket and scribbled onto a napkin.

"Was he doing anything else when you saw him?"

"The first time, he was sitting on a bench, and I swear he was watching me."

Declan pulled out his phone, tapped on the screen, then held it to his ear. After a moment, he spoke. "Brad, it's Dex. Can you run this plate for me?" He read it from the napkin. "I'll hold."

After a long minute where Declan's gaze remained steadily on her, he bent his head to listen, then said, "Anything else? Okay, got it. Thanks."

He set down his phone, expression thoughtful. "The car is registered to a private investigator out of Santa Cruz by the name of David Portillo. Ring any bells for you?"

She could feel the blood drain from her face. "No." But she knew what the presence of a private investigator, especially one from Santa Cruz, meant. "Julius must have hired him."

"That's a good bet."

"And he's seen us together, and with your license plate he'll be able to find out who you are and where you live." She stared out the window while she fought to control the hysteria that wanted to rise up and choke her. "You said there's a motel in town, where is it?"

"The Bluebird? Down at the end of Main, why?"

"I'll get a room there for the night."

"Why the hell would you do that?"

"Because he'll know who you are. He could come after you. You're not safe if I'm there with you." Her hands gripped the edge of the table, the food in front of her forgotten.

"Fuck that."

"That's hardly a reasoned response."

"Neither is yours."

"I am being reasonable. We need to get back to the cabin. I'll get my stuff and get a room at the motel." She paused. "I want my ammo back."

"Jesus Christ, Meghan." He leaned forward. "There's no way in hell I'll let you go now."

Not sure what he meant by that, she tried another tack. "Maybe it would be better to go to the police chief today. Waiting until tomorrow only delays the inevitable. I think Chief Gallagher will have to make time for me."

He reached across the table to pry one hand from its death grip on the table edge. Holding it firmly in his, his thumb caressing her palm, he said, "Listen carefully. You're not going anywhere but with me back to the cabin where you'll stay exactly like we'd planned. I can damn well protect you from an asshole like Portillo. My experience with PIs is that they play it safe. They gather information but aren't inclined to put themselves in danger for a client."

He must have sensed her tension. He raised her hand to brush his lips over her knuckles and melted her heart. "I talked to Brad and he says to come see him tomorrow. You're safe with me, Meghan." He motioned to her plate. "We'll finish our lunch, then go."

***

Julius Merritt leaned back on the wicker chaise, gazing out at his own little slice of well-deserved paradise. His home sat on a bluff above the Pacific Ocean, a view that cost him well over four million dollars to acquire. He drew in on the blunt, allowing the view and the cannabis to relax him, chasing it with the easy burn of fine bourbon. The price of the home was expected. Successful, brilliant people deserved the best, and he'd earned the standard of living he'd come to enjoy. That didn't mean he didn't have compassion for those less than him. He took great satisfaction in slipping a twenty into some beggar's hand, and he didn't think it was wrong that he carried hand sanitizer and used it liberally afterward.

People didn't understand the precautions being famous forced him to take. He couldn't walk down a street or into a store. Strangers recognized him, wanted pictures with him, wanted to take a little of his fame for themselves. He understood their desire—who wouldn't want to share in the glow of the brightest star in the sky? He really hated when he had to turn them down.

Lately there had been nasty voices on social media who repeated the ugliness suggesting his shine was tarnishing. Didn't they know of the talk that he was on the short list for a Nobel Prize in medicine? He sipped his drink. So what if he'd started that rumor himself. The Nobel committee needed a little nudge. Then that *LA Times* article had come out, made him out to be nothing more than a grifter, a *con* man who violated the trust people placed in the medical devices he created. It gave him some small satisfaction to know the writer of that shit piece had suffered serious injury in an automobile accident that wasn't really an accident. Payback could be quite satisfying.

One big drawback of being rich enough, powerful enough to buy the common man a few thousand times over, however, was having to allow some people access to him. He was always uncomfortable with the fact that he was forced to rely on the people who worked for him. He paid them handsomely, more than enough to ensure their loyalty. Or so he'd thought.

Hiring Meg Bennett had been a regrettable mistake. He had permitted her to get close. She'd lived in his home, for god's sake, then had betrayed that trust in the most ruthless fashion. Such disloyalty could never be forgiven. She would have to be punished.

A subtle chime signaled an incoming message. He grabbed his phone and opened the email. Finally. Portillo pissed him off, dithering about going over the mountains because of a little weather. Then the idiot had elected to drive hundreds of miles out of the way to take a more southerly route and avoid the snow. Now, finally, he claimed he'd located her. Better have, or the private investigator wouldn't be paid a dime.

Julius scrolled down to the photos. Meg getting out of a four-wheel-drive vehicle, walking along a wooden sidewalk in some loser town. Another of her at a park of some sort, a lake in the background. Finding her hadn't been all that hard. Shouldn't have been, because he'd attached a GPS tracker inside the tire well of her vehicle as soon as she'd begun working for him.

But ever since he'd learned of her betrayal, he'd suspected she'd had help from someone, and now he knew for sure. He squinted at the unfocused image of a tall, bearded man exiting the same vehicle, then another of them entering a restaurant together. When he'd researched Meg's background before hiring her, there'd been no evidence of a boyfriend. He wondered how she'd slipped that by him.

He squinted again at the photo. Portillo really did take shitty pictures. But even with the grainy quality, the man looked familiar. He took a puff on the joint and studied the image, scanned the next message that came through. He stilled, then reread it as his vision began hazing to red.

He inhaled the smoke deeply into his lungs, letting his breath out slowly. It didn't help to dispel the swelling anger that had the blood pounding in his ears. He read the report on the man Meg was with and seethed. Declan Michael Murphy. His hands shook. Meg must have been a plant sent by Murphy. There was no other explanation. The report gave the basics. Murphy was a decorated Los Angeles PD veteran, recently retired at the rank of lieutenant after being injured in the line of duty. He'd been assigned to a division that investigated human trafficking. Blah, blah, fucking blah.

The fury slid in fast as it always did, that instantaneous spike of rage that even the marijuana couldn't soften. Julius leapt to his feet, not recognizing the obscenities bellowing from his mouth as his own. Shattering the lowball glass against the stone wall didn't ease the fury, so he grabbed the glass-topped table and flung it with all his might. Shards of glass flew from the destroyed table, and when his cheek stung, he wiped it to find blood staining his fingers.

He *hated* Declan Murphy. Loathed the lowlife scum who didn't deserve to breathe the same air as him. For his entire adult life, whenever he was thwarted or disrespected, Julius always made it a practice to balance his own personal scales of justice in a manner that suited him, but he'd never been able to touch the bastard Murphy.

Memories rampaged through his head until he wanted to scream. That the conflict between them had happened so long ago was of no consequence. Over the years Julius had evaluated and discarded the best method of vengeance but hadn't settled on one he thought would properly punish Murphy and still allow Julius to remain free of any possible association with said punishment.

That Murphy had never paid after so smugly arresting him, *humiliating* him, all those years before was a constant source of pain for Julius. For nearly fifteen years, no plan he could come up with had been worthy as retribution for that affront, so he'd bided his time, followed the fucker's career, and patiently waited for the moment when payback would be most rewarding.

Now he had evidence of Meg's involvement with the bastard. That they had succeeded in tricking him into allowing Meg to live in his house and have access not only to his person, but to the inner workings of his business, threatened to send him into another paroxysm of rage.

Then the thought struck like a stroke of lightning, blinding in its brilliance. He could get them both, Meg Bennett and Declan Murphy, with the same axe of vengeance. The plan unfolded in his mind, helping to lessen the rage. He lit another joint and felt calm return. There was even a little regret at the destruction he'd wrought on the patio furniture.

He brushed glass from the chaise to lie down again and returned his attention to his phone to study the PI's report on Murphy.

Julius had always resented all the praise and hoopla heaped on *first responders*. Even that title irked him. Police, firefighters, rescue teams, they were peons like anyone else who punched a timecard. The true heroes were people like him who used their minds to create life-saving devices.

But the media, politicians, police organizations, they all manipulated the public with their hyped-up stories of heroism and courage. They roiled Julius's gut and made him want to vomit. Not long after Murphy had arrested him in the most humiliating fashion, the fucker had been all over the news again, this time when he'd pulled an idiot teenager out of a rip current at the beach. Lifeguards had been busy keeping another stupid kid from drowning, and the media had fawned all over the off-duty cop.

The worst part was that some assholes had found and recirculated images on social media from when Murphy had arrested him when Julius had been a student at USC, further embarrassing him and renewing his rage with all the "Hunk and the Drunk" crap.

The fawning attention paid to Murphy made Julius sick. But now he understood why he'd never moved ahead with a plan for revenge. A divine hand had held him back, that much was obvious, and his patience had been rewarded because now he would get both Declan Murphy and Meg Bennett with one righteous act of retribution.

Julius didn't really care if Meg and the cop were getting it on. He'd expected better of her, but whatever. What he did care about was getting back his own. His own personal failing was that he trusted too easily.

He'd expected Meg's loyalty and it hurt that she'd been playing him the entire time. Not only had she stolen from him but, a much more egregious offense, she'd drugged him. That night he'd awoken to find himself laid out on the terrace floor, his head aching so badly he'd screamed violently in pain. He'd yelled for Meg, repeatedly, but she hadn't come.

One of the maids had called nine-one-one. The bumbling, incompetent EMTs had claimed he'd overdosed. Since he'd been careful to nurture a relationship with the city manager, he'd pulled hard on that string to keep the emergency call hush-hush. A blood test had revealed alcohol, but more interestingly, a high level of diazepam. The bitch had somehow slipped him Valium.

Meg's betrayal extended beyond himself. When she'd stolen from his accounts, she'd taken money entrusted to him by investors to create and market devices that saved human lives. The social media trolls who trashed him with accusations that those devices were killing patients were just that, trolls spewing out their vile lies.

Since it was a personal point of pride, he'd had his tech team tracking those trolls, rooting them out, hacking their accounts, and making sure payback destroyed their little worlds.

That Meg Bennett not only stole from him but had violated his person with an overdose of drugs meant vengeance for her would be appropriately severe. Usually, he let a few chosen employees dispense justice for him, and the deserving victims never knew that he'd been the architect of whatever form of payback he'd chosen. But this time he would take care of business himself. He wanted them to know he was the mastermind of their misery.

He would recover the money Meg had stolen, retrieve the copies of the files he was sure she had made, and then mete out the punishment both she and Murphy deserved. The idea that justice would finally be served brought a measure of peace. He'd have to come up with a plan suitably elegant for his tastes, and he wouldn't kill them unless forced to.

He wasn't a murderer. He was more civilized than that. Maybe he could even manage to manipulate one of them into a nice little murder/suicide. If they chose to end their own lives, well that was hardly his fault.

Pulling up Google maps, he put in the address revealed by the GPS tracker. He'd get a couple of hours sleep, then get an early start on his drive over the mountains.

Chapter Ten

"Why do you have your niece's cat?"

Dex relaxed back in his chair, the cat a warm heap on his lap. A cold longneck bottle of Hangman's Lager rested on his knee. Meghan sat across from him on the couch, feet curled beneath her, dark hair a cloud of curls around her head. Too damned appealing, as far as he was concerned. She looked at him expectantly, her hands wrapped around a mug of tea.

He took a sip of his beer. "The kid was convinced I'd be lonely up here on my own. She insisted I bring the cat with me. It's impossible to say no to her."

"That's sweet. She gave you a therapy cat."

He stroked the cat. "I've gotten used to her."

"Why aren't you a cop any longer? You act like one. You think like one. What happened?"

"Nothing exciting."

"Maybe not to you. You don't know what excites me." She put up her hand even as he grinned. "Stop that. I wasn't being suggestive."

"Too bad."

"Now you're being suggestive."

"You started it."

"No, *you* started it this morning with that kiss."

"I'll accept that. It was a good kiss. Excellent, in fact. Wanna do it again?"

"We are not going to make out on the couch and we're not talking about that kiss. We're talking about why you're not a cop. Don't deflect, Declan Murphy."

"Jesus, I should never have told you my last name. You sound like my fifth-grade teacher." He rubbed a hand over his face and down his beard. He stroked BC, eliciting a gentle purr. He stared into the fire hissing and crackling in the fireplace. Meghan didn't say a word, and he had the idea she was simply waiting him out.

His ex-wife hadn't wanted the gritty details of his experiences as a cop, so he'd gotten in the habit of not sharing, of locking away the ugliness he saw on a daily basis so it couldn't pollute the rest of his life. But he'd been fooling himself, because he had still let the weight of it affect him. He finally returned his attention to Meghan. Keeping emotional distance from her was getting harder and harder when nearly everything about her appealed to him. Her looks, her clever mind, and the way she'd turn those blue eyes on him, which made him feel like he was the most important person in her world. Maybe they were starting something together and he really could talk to her.

"I had to get out. I was with the LAPD human trafficking division, and I was becoming too cynical. I wasn't liking myself."

"Human trafficking? That must have been hard, dealing with the worst people doing despicable things."

"I did see the worst, and the victims. Women and children who'd been abducted and were enslaved with no means of escape. Dealing with that level of depravity every day eats at you."

"Was there a single event that forced your decision, or a buildup of many?"

He didn't intend to tell her, was going to change the conversation to something less serious, but when he opened his mouth, the memories spilled out. "Both. The busts where you're pulling a john off a twelve-year-old, and it takes everything you have not to beat him to a bloody pulp. The rooms with teenage girls who'd come from south of the border and believed the lies that they were going to work as models, who still believed it even as their pimps sold them to perverted old men. Those added up." He stared into the fire, seeing the young faces in the flames. He guessed telling her was a kind of test for them both. If she covered her ears and metaphorically stuck her head in the sand, he'd know that, like his relationship with his ex-wife, he had to keep it superficial between them.

"I can't imagine how horrific it must have been for those girls. Or for you. It's good that you caught some of the monsters who did that to them, but it must have been difficult to realize that the victims would wear the scars from their experiences for the rest of their lives."

He appreciated her insight, her willingness to listen. Rather than pushing him away, she appeared to be genuinely trying to understand, to make sense of the world that had been his. He was more than a little surprised that having Meghan listen eased something inside him, made the ghosts of his past a bit easier to live with.

"You're right. But there are some good people who run programs to help them, and legal organizations that volunteer to deal with the immigration issues."

"And the big event that pushed you to quit? Does it have to do with your leg injury?"

He stopped rubbing his thigh. "Yeah." He was silent, staring into the fire. He'd done the department-mandated counseling, but since then had gotten used to not talking about that moment when evil had worn the face of a cop.

Meghan knew how to wait, compassion flowing from her like heat from the fire, warm and soothing.

Even with that, he surprised himself when he started telling her. "There was a new guy in our division, hired from another agency. Came out later that the other department had let him quit after misconduct rather than give him a bad review. He had some family connections that let him skate. Guy's name was Kenneth Cunningham, nicknamed Redneck, because that's what he was. I didn't really like him personally but had to deal. Cops work together, depend on each other, risk their lives, so you trust them. It's the only way you can function on the job. We were a tight group. And despite being an asshole more than occasionally, Cunningham did his job. At least he seemed to." Dex stretched out his leg to ease the ache.

"What happened?"

He sipped his beer, swallowed before answering. "Shit wasn't adding up. I began to suspect he was on the take. I went to my captain, who started an investigation. It all came to a head when I recorded audio of Cunningham getting paid off by a pimp."

She set her tea mug carefully on the end table, eyes round when she looked back at him. "How did you get a recording? That must have been dangerous."

He shrugged. "It was amazingly easy. Our captain assigned us as partners. I set my phone to record and slid it down between the seat and the center console. We were in an unmarked department car. I had Cunningham drop me off somewhere, and he did what I'd figured he'd do, he took the opportunity to hook up with the pimp. I recovered my phone a couple hours later and it was all there, corruption at its finest."

"And the injury?"

The memory brought a restlessness that had him sitting forward in the chair, elbows on his knees. For a moment he braced his head in his hands. When he looked up again, Meghan's steady gaze eased the tightness in his gut.

"I played the recording for the captain. What I'd gotten seemed pretty damning, but he said we needed more. So we set the fucker up. We knew who the pimp was, that he was expecting a van carrying a group of girls from across the border. When Cunningham asked for the day off, we figured we had him. We set up the sting." The memories sucked him back into that blazing hot afternoon, the frightened young women in the back of the van, the sharp crack of gunfire followed by the stench of burnt cordite.

"It started off as planned, then went sideways too damn fast. Turns out Cunningham wasn't amenable to being arrested. Gun fight, then boom, I'm on my back bleeding out in the parking lot of a scumbag motel. Luckily the cavalry came, got me onto a chopper. Upshot, the pimp was dead, and I had a ball of lead hugging my femoral artery. But the women were rescued, and we got Cunningham. He's in prison serving a twenty-year-to-life sentence."

"Jesus, Declan. You could have died."

"Could have, but didn't. Docs operated. Guess it was dicey for a while, being that the slug was so close to a major artery. There was some tissue damage. I had a lot of time to think while recovering."

"And you decided you didn't want to be a cop anymore."

"Yeah. Sounds sappy, but I felt like I was losing myself to the cynicism of the job. I took some of that time sitting in the rehab facility to finish a manuscript I'd been working on. A friend got me in touch with another friend who connected me with someone who knew an agent. Agent liked what she read, agreed to represent me, and sold the book."

"For the record, it doesn't sound sappy to me. And that's awesome about the book. You wrote while you were a cop?"

"Yeah. My wife never wanted to hear about the job, my friends were cops and we talked some, but not anything real personal. Everything went onto the page and it seemed to help me keep my shit together, and people bought the book."

"It's already out? Really? Are you using a pseudonym?"

"Dex Michaels."

She sat up abruptly. "Dex Michaels? You're Dex Michaels?"

"You've read the book?"

"No, but it's on my TBR list, already loaded on my Kindle. *Hail of Bullets* got a lot of attention when it came out. You earned some awards."

"I did. But better than that, it got me the contract for the next book."

"I seem to remember that all proceeds from the purchase are donated to charity." She narrowed her eyes. "Let me guess, a charity that helps victims of human trafficking."

He shifted uncomfortably. "Yeah, maybe." The cat jumped down and trotted to the couch to leap onto the cushion and settle next to Meg.

"You're a good man, Declan Murphy."

He rubbed the ache in his thigh, stopping when he saw her following the movement.

"Does it hurt all the time?"

"Not all the time, and it's better now than it was."

Even knowing it was a stupid move, he pushed to his feet. Skirting the coffee table, he booted the cat to take her spot next to Meg. Not looking at her, he took her hand in his. Turning it over, he used a forefinger to trace the crease in her palm, then up the slender underside of her wrist.

"You have delicate bones."

He turned his head and found her studying their joined hands like they held the secrets to the universe. When she raised her gaze to his, he saw a vulnerability he hadn't expected, a vulnerability that pulled at his heart.

"What are we doing here, Declan?" The words were uttered softly.

"Damned if I know. But I'll say it right out front in case it's relevant—I suck at relationships."

She raised her free hand and traced the skin along his cheekbone, above his beard, and had his blood stirring hotter at the same time as it felt like brittle ice surrounding his heart was forming deep cracks.

"I doubt that. Unless being honest is a failing in a relationship."

"How do you know I'm honest in relationships?"

"I've known you for two days, and that's been long enough to figure out you're the most honest person I know. If you don't want to say what you're thinking, you don't say anything. But what you do say is the truth."

Her words brought a flash of guilt. She was wrong. Honesty was high on his list of key character traits, but he hadn't been honest with Meghan. Extenuating circumstances didn't excuse the fact that he hadn't disclosed information she deserved to know. "Here's honesty for you. I want you, and not only for one night." He pressed his lips to the pulse beating at her wrist.

She drew in a sharp breath, then cupped her hand around his jaw. Eyes open and watchful, she brought her lips to his, testing, teasing, as the tension built. He leaned in, dove deeper. Lips, tongues, teeth met in a delicious clash of want and need. The kiss spun out and Dex let himself feel in ways he hadn't in far too long.

Going with the need, he wrapped an arm around her waist and moved with her until they were lying on the couch. He nibbled on her chin as she lay back, legs open as he settled in exactly where he wanted to be.

"Make love to me, Declan." The whispered words slid around his brain like a magician's spell.

He framed her face with his hands. "Tell me this isn't because you think you're going to jail tomorrow and you figure it's a one-shot deal. I want more than that from you."

He felt more than heard her laughing. She slapped a hand over her mouth to stifle a giggle.

"Something funny?"

She moved her hand to speak. "One-shot deal?" she sputtered. "Is that all you've got? I was hoping for more staying power than that."

"One-shot, my ass." With a growl, he bit at the curve of her neck.

She tilted her pelvis to press more intimately against the bulge straining the material of his jeans. "Evidence does suggest more than one shot is a strong possibility."

He groaned. He couldn't help it. She was rubbing against him in the most erotic way and all he wanted to do was strip her down and plunge in. He pushed off the couch, reaching down to haul her up over his shoulder, her squeal of protest nearly deafening him. With his hand on her ass to secure her, he made for the stairs.

"Wait. What are you doing?"

"Lugging you to my bedroom. You said we weren't making out on the couch, so that leaves my bed. Plus, that's where the condoms are. An entire box of them, in case we go more than the one shot."

She braced her hands on his back. "You might not even get that one shot. In case you're too dense, this is *not* romantic. Sweeping me off my feet, carrying me upstairs in your arms, that's romance. Lugging me over your shoulder like a bag of dog food? Not so much."

He chuckled. "Duck your head, the ceiling's low up here."

***

Meg ducked, heart thudding in her ears. His bad leg sure didn't prevent him from climbing the stairs with ease. She wiggled and his hand clamped down harder on her rear. "Hold still." God, that gruff and gravelly voice made her girl parts want to stand up and salute.

They reached the landing, barely illuminated by a nightlight, and he let her slip down his chest, catching her to cradle her in his arms.

"This more romantic?"

"You bet." He held her with ease, biceps bulging under the knit shirt he wore. She opened her mouth to speak, and whatever she'd intended to say vanished from her brain because as soon as her lips parted, his mouth claimed hers in a kiss both sumptuous and steaming.

With his powerful arms supporting her, she slid her hands across his broad shoulders, fingers diving into that thick hair, not quite brown, not quite black, and reveled in the freedom to touch and feel to her heart's content.

When he moved, she wrapped her legs around his waist, lips still clinging to his as he walked them into the darkened bedroom. He laid her on the bedspread and she tightened her legs to keep him locked against her. He groaned, low and throaty, and then eased onto her.

His lips and tongue traced a fiery trail from her mouth to her ear, then down to her breasts, nuzzling aside the cardigan she wore. He shifted back, but only so he could lift the thin t-shirt under the sweater to expose the skin of her belly.

Going by feel, she slid her hands under his shirt, skimming over long muscles and the ridges of his spine.

"You've got too many clothes on," he muttered, tugging off the cardigan.

"Have I? It seemed like a good idea this morning."

"That was then," he muttered as worked off the t-shirt, tossing it off the bed. "This is now."

Her response morphed into a long, drawn-out moan when he ran his tongue under her bra and found her nipple. She pulled aside the cup to give him better access and this time the low groan came from him. He feasted, savored, used his tongue to explore, moving from one breast to the other. One-handed, he managed to undo the clasp and pull the bra off her shoulders without leaving her breasts unattended.

Finally he released her to prop himself on his elbow, stretching an arm to turn on the lamp on the nightstand. He stopped her instinctive move to cover her breasts, his big hand enfolding hers. "Don't hide from me. Your breasts are beautiful. You're beautiful."

"Seems like I'm the only one undressed here."

"Not undressed enough, but we can remedy that."

Determined to overcome her shyness, she said, "My turn," and tugged his shirt up and over his head. He lay on his back and she took the opportunity to explore the wide expanse of his chest. Broad pectoral muscles, flat belly, dark hair that arrowed down to disappear under his belt. She let her fingers glide through the wiry hair over his chest, a few silvered strands glinting in the light.

"How old are you?"

"Thirty-eight. That too old for you?"

"Hardly. I'm thirty-two."

"Good," he grunted. "You look like you're about twenty-five, which is too young."

She found a thin scar about two inches long on his right side, beneath his ribs. Tracing it, she asked, "What is this from?"

"Stupidity."

Even as one hand rested on his belt buckle, she lowered her lips to the marred skin. "Explain," she ordered quietly as she kissed the mark, then let her lips track lower.

"I, ah…" He seemed to be having trouble finding words, making her smile. "I was seventeen and thought I could hurdle a barbed wire fence. I couldn't."

"I see," she murmured. She'd managed to get his belt undone, and then his fly, and when she was ready to follow the path of newly revealed skin with her mouth, he hitched her up to lie over him.

"Did I mention it's been a long time?"

"No."

"It's been a long time, long enough that if you take your mouth where you were taking it, I'd be over and done with before we get started."

She couldn't help the amusement that crept into her voice. "You talking about the one-shot deal?"

He growled. "Let's just say we're not starting off with a single shot. We're going for double-barrels."

The laugh rolled out of her. "I'm guessing 'double-barrels' is code for simultaneous orgasms?"

"Damn straight it is."

"Now I'm intrigued."

"I'll intrigue you, all right." In a swift move, he had her on her back. He snugged a pillow under her head, quickly shucked his jeans, then tugged and yanked to get her pants off. Starting with his hands traveling up the inner curve of her thighs, he set about touching and tasting until her body heated to a fever peak. Eyes closed tight, the sensations he elicited created a spectrum of color behind her eyelids, a kaleidoscope of patterns forming and reforming.

Feeling his erection prodding her hip, she reached for him, her hand closing around the hardness encased in silk. "I'm ready for your barrel now."

She could feel the laugh shudder out of him even as he groaned. He kissed her lips, then muttered, "One sec."

With her eyes still closed, her sense of hearing heightened. There was the sliding sound of the drawer opening, the crinkle of a foil packet, a brief moment of quiet, and then he was nestled, hard against soft, and all she could think was, *finally*. She lifted to take him in, the initial entry nearly pushing her to climax. Her eyes fluttered open to find his fixed on her with penetrating concentration. Then he closed his eyes, pressed his lips to hers, and began moving in long, delicious strokes.

Over and over in a steady rhythm, in tandem as if they'd done this a hundred times, they moved together. The Hallelujah chorus echoed in her mind because she was there, building with him, their motion speeding to the crescendo, then exploding into a mind-numbing finale. His body, released like an arrow from a bow, sagged against her, breath hot against her neck.

"I told you we'd get both barrels," he muttered into her hair. He held her as she laughed in his ear, then pulled her with him when he shifted his weight off her until they were lying on their sides still joined.

"Give me a couple minutes, and we'll see if we can dispel any single-shot worries."

Chapter Eleven

The cat jumping onto the bed woke Meg. She opened her eyes to find the darkness of night had lifted to a dull gray, suggesting a cloudy morning. The master bedroom boasted large windows, and the blinds were angled to let in the light. She nudged Declan over. No holding her tenderly through the night for this guy. He lay sprawled on his stomach, taking up most of the bed. Even with the chill in the night air he slept shirtless, the sheet pushed down to his waist. The temptation was strong to stroke that broad back, to wake him in the most interesting of ways, and see how he liked making love in the morning. That he'd already proven himself to be a three-shot kind of guy, and that she'd matched him shot for shot, had her feeling a little smug.

Buttercup padded over the blankets to thrust her head under Meg's hand, already purring. She pet the ginger and black fur, finally letting the thoughts she'd been holding at bay roll to the forefront of her mind. Yesterday had been a wonderful, almost idyllic reprieve, but today she had to face reality. Jail, trial, prison—that was her future. Whatever was developing between her and Declan would grow cold with her absence, dying embers in a neglected hearth.

Calling herself a fool, she wiped at her eyes with the edge of the sheet, and slipped from the bed, going to her room to retrieve clean clothes. She planned to shower, pack her bags, have breakfast with Declan, then go into town to meet with the police chief. The flash drive was secure in the side pocket of her duffel bag and she'd need to retrieve it before going into town.

Walking into the shower, she turned the faucets, waiting and wondering how much time she'd have to spend in jail. Meg tipped back her head, eyes screwed shut, and let the hot water beat over her, refusing to think how horrible prison showers were likely to be. She gave a startled yelp when the curtain yanked back. Declan stepped under the spray, frown in place.

He framed her face in his hands, brows lowered. "You've been crying."

She didn't bother denying it. "Yeah, I have."

He was aroused and she expected him to make good on that promise, but he continued to study her, thumbs brushing over her cheekbones. He lowered his lips to hers in a kiss so tender it made her heart ache.

"Don't, Declan. Please, don't. I don't want to fall in love with you." Her voice shook.

"Could you?"

Afraid of the answer, she didn't speak. Instead, she reached for him, closing soapy hands around his erection and eliciting a rumbling growl from deep in his chest. They made love in the close confines of the steamy shower, coming together with an intensity that held an edge of desperation.

***

Meg chewed her thumbnail as she looked over her belongings. She hadn't really thought it through, but she felt sure she wouldn't be able to take her things with her when she went to jail. She knew cell phones were prohibited, but what about laptops if they weren't connected to the internet? And what should she do with her father's pistol? Would she be able to bring her own bras and underwear? A noise behind her had her turning her head.

Declan leaned against the doorframe of the little bedroom. He wore a dark brown Henley and rugged canvas work pants. "Ready to go?"

"Without repeating your mantra that I'm not going to jail, do you know if inmates are allowed to take personal belongings?"

"Depends on the prison."

"Great, that's no help."

"Okay, theoretically speaking, let's say Brad or the district attorney decides they're not only going to arrest you, which is unlikely, but you also don't make bail. If that happened, I would keep your belongings here, including your car. And if you were allowed to have any of them, I would bring them to you." He gestured to her belongings. "We don't need to take any of this with us today."

She nodded slowly. "I hate to put all that on you, but thank you. Do you plan to stay at the cabin? I don't want to leave it uninhabited."

"Yeah, I plan to stay here. Your things are safe, and the cabin will be looked after. But it doesn't matter, because you're not going to jail."

***

Why did it feel like time was racing? Gray clouds hung heavy in the sky, and as they'd driven down the mountain road a fine rain had begun to fall. A stiff breeze whipped up white caps on the lake and sent crows wheeling in the sky. The gloomy weather matched Meg's mood perfectly.

Although she'd taken in the scenery as they made their way into town, it seemed that she'd blinked and Declan was pulling the 4Runner into the parking lot of the Hangman's Loss Police Department.

She stepped out of the vehicle, mentally squaring her shoulders against what was to come. Declan took her hand, twining his fingers with hers as they walked to the wide glass double doors. Once inside they stopped at a reception counter where a woman sat working yarn the color of cranberries with a crochet hook.

"Declan Murphy and Meghan Bennett, we're here to see Brad," Declan told the woman. "We're expecting Brenda Nguyen to join us."

"Sure thing." The woman set aside the square she was crocheting and picked up the phone. "Chief, there are folks to see you. Handsome here," she winked at Declan, "says their names are Declan Murphy and Meghan Bennett. You want me to send them back?" She listened for a moment longer, then replied, "Okay, then." and set the phone back on its cradle. "Chief says he'll come up in a sec. Brenda's not here yet, but I'll send her back when she gets in."

She picked up her yarn again, and a minute later a tall man with a rangy build strode from the back of the building. Meg had expected a full chief's uniform, maybe with a lot of stripes on the sleeve, but this guy wore sturdy Carhartt pants with his badge and gun attached to a cop belt, His chambray shirt had the sleeves rolled back past his elbows. He had direct green eyes and exuded a calm, steady authority.

The night before, as Meg and Declan had lain curled into each other after making love, Declan explained his history with Chief Bradley Gallagher. He told her how about Brad's wife, Emma, and had how when she'd come to town and reopened the cabins that she'd been targeted by violent, unscrupulous people, and that Brad had been shot protecting her. Maddy, at the café, was Brad's sister, and while her husband Logan was now with the sheriff's department, at the time he had been with the FBI working on a dangerous case. Brad had asked for Declan's assistance when Maddy had been kidnapped.

Brad tipped his head in Declan's direction and uttered a casual, "Dex." Then he stretched out a hand to Meg. "Meghan, I'm Brad Gallagher. I hear you have a story to tell me."

Meg shook his hand, then returned to twisting the strap of her purse. "I do, and please call me Meg."

"Do you want Dex present for the telling?"

"If you don't mind. And Brenda Nguyen will be joining us."

"I don't mind. I'll show you to the conference room. Can I get either of you coffee or a soda?"

Meg shook her head, sure anything in her stomach wouldn't sit well. Declan nodded. "Coffee for me, black."

The crocheting lady chirped, "I'll get that, Chief," and followed after them.

Declan and Meg sat side by side at a long table. Brad came in a moment later, the no-nonsense Brenda Nguyen following him.

Brad set a pad of paper and pen on the desk, and drew a small black device from his shirt pocket. "If it's all right with you and your lawyer, Meg, I'd like to record this meeting."

Meg glanced at her attorney, and at her nod, said, "That's fine."

Brad spoke into the recorder, giving the date and time, and naming everyone present, then set it in the middle of the table. "Meg, while you tell me your story, I'm going to write questions down as they come to me. I may stop you every now and then to ask for clarification or elaboration, but I'll keep my interruptions to a minimum."

Meg drew in a deep, calming breath, let it out, and started. It helped that Declan was on her side, and that her lawyer was there for her too. Telling the story was easier than Meg thought it would be. Brad listened, his steadiness helping her to focus and relate what had happened in a logical manner. He stopped her when she recounted how she'd been downloading files when Julius had come in the house after meeting with the Chinese businessman, George Liu.

"At what point were you aware Merritt was misrepresenting the success of his devices?"

She leaned back in her seat, trying to pinpoint when she'd gone from believing Julius to realizing he was lying. "To write his biography, I had to interview him extensively, and things began to unravel. The stories of his childhood up through his teenage years were heavily interspersed with anecdotes where he'd describe selfless or heroic acts he claimed to have done. But then he'd contradict himself, and when I questioned him he'd blow up and accuse me of twisting his words, of being disloyal.

"Loyalty is important to Julius. But I wasn't wrong. He couldn't keep his stories straight. Then we got to the part in the book where we were writing about the medical devices, and I needed extra information, so he gave me access to everything, all the research, all the reports from the professors who did the research, documents from the FDA. The first devices he created were successful, there is no question about that. But I think that success fed what I guess is his god complex."

Brad tapped his pen on the notepad. "Why would he give you access to information that was potentially harmful to him? Wouldn't he want to cover that up?"

"You'd think, but if you don't believe you've done anything wrong, that it's even possible for you to do anything wrong, then you have nothing to hide.

"Julius believes he's brilliant, and that everything he touches is golden. When the report from the researchers came back that the device was leading to an unacceptable number of deaths, Julius accused them of lying and trying to destroy his reputation so they could pass the device off as their own. He wanted to launch in Asia with positive outcomes in his pocket, which meant he planned to cherry-pick his results so he'd be able to demonstrate success to his backers." She glanced at Declan, found his dark gaze reassuring, and continued. "The thing is, some of the research results sent to investors had been falsified, and they originated from my email account and were sent from my personal laptop."

"Did you send them?"

"No. I'll admit I was in a fog after my dad died, but I would never have made that kind of mistake. There's no way I falsified the reports. I don't have the knowledge to change test results and make them look realistic, and I would never have sent false reports to those investors."

"And your plan once you copied his files?"

"A week or so before I left, I took a group of files I'd found to the police. They said they'd look into it. When I didn't hear back, I called and was told there wasn't enough evidence in what I'd given them. That's why I was copying more files."

"Where did you store the files?"

She tugged on the chain she'd put back around her neck, pulling the flash drive from under her shirt. "They're all here."

Brad produced an envelope, scribbled notes on the outside, and slipped the flash drive inside. She gave him the password, then signed the receipt listing what property she was turning over to the police department. She hadn't expected the feeling of relief she had once it was off her hands.

"Anything else?" Brad gave her a questioning look.

"There's the money." So far, what she'd told him could be excused because she'd taken files that would expose Julius's wrongdoing. But taking the money had a different feel to it. "I embezzled almost a million dollars that investors had given Julius to fund his research and the marketing of the medical devices."

Brad leaned back in his chair and Meg had the feeling she'd just spoken the words that would land her in jail.

"Tell me more."

She related the same information she'd given Declan. When she was done, Brad said, "It seems you could have left with the files with the intent of turning them over to law enforcement and been protected by whistleblower laws, but taking the money is going to be problematic for you."

Brenda spoke up. "My client didn't take the money for her own gain. In fact, she donated it for a social good."

Brad nodded to the lawyer. "Everyone at this table knows that doesn't excuse the theft." He directed his next question to Meg. "What was your motivation for taking the money?"

"Julius would have used that money to continue production on devices that were killing people. I wanted to prevent that. Honestly, the idea popped into my head, and I went with it. I found a website that lists women who need money for important social causes or to help their communities in a real tangible way. Most of the grants are for fairly small amounts. It's amazing that a few hundred dollars would help dig a well in Africa, and can have such a huge impact for the people living there. So that's what I did with it." No matter what happened, Meg wouldn't regret that she'd sent the money to people who would use it for a positive good.

Brad leaned forward. "Tell me about the events leading up to your decision to put crushed Valium tablets in Mr. Merritt's drink."

Meg drew a deep breath, and when she'd regained some measure of calm, told him the rest of the story. At the end, she explained, "He hit me, and I felt threatened. I don't think he would have simply let me leave."

"You felt your life was in danger."

"Absolutely. He was becoming more and more controlling, keeping me busy, requiring I attend events that I really didn't need to be at. That was all so I wouldn't have time to see my mom or friends. When I did manage to get away for a few hours, I swear he had spies in town, because he'd ask how I liked the restaurant I'd been at with my mom, or if I'd enjoyed the water at the beach. I took four days to get here because I wanted to lose anyone he might have had following me."

Declan sat up. "Wait a minute. You think he was tracking your movements?"

"Not exactly. It's pretty obvious if I went to the beach, because there would be sandy towels and beach things, but I don't see how he knew what restaurant I'd met my mom at, or how he knew that my friend Andrea and I had gotten together and driven into Monterey."

Declan looked at Brad, who nodded.

"What?"

"When we get back to the cabin, we're searching your car," Declan said.

"For what?"

"A tracking device. I bet the fucker put a GPS tracker on your car, or in something you have with you all the time, like your purse. Most likely your car, though."

Brad nodded. "He's right. I'll go with you to look."

***

If Julius was going to come out on top, and he would, it was simply a matter of being smarter than everyone else. He thought through his options and chose the best one. A smart man wouldn't go right up to the shoddy little cabin and park next to Meg's car, so he'd driven by slowly and determined no one was home. Muddy tire tracks in the driveway showing a vehicle had recently departed, likely the SUV Murphy drove, confirmed Julius's belief. Up the road a bit was another long driveway with patches of dirty snow melting under the incessant drizzle. The house at the end of the drive had no evidence that anyone had been there in months, so he reasoned he could park his car without risking Meg seeing the Mercedes. He should have rented a car so there'd be no chance she'd recognize his vehicle, but he'd left Santa Cruz early in the morning and none of the rental places had been open. That left him parking in the middle of the godforsaken forest so his car wouldn't be identified. He hated the idea of tramping around in the woods, but it couldn't be helped.

He set out, wanting to do a quick search of the cabin before anyone returned. He moved quickly, slipping in the slushy snow. If he'd known he would be out in the elements, he would have packed the appropriate clothing, but he hadn't and now his feet were wet and freezing, his hands were numb, and he was already panting heavily. Since he worked out regularly in his home gym to keep in prime condition, the heavy breathing was likely the result of having climbed over eight thousand feet in altitude in one day.

The cabin came into view between the trees. Maybe he'd get lucky and Murphy had left a door unlocked or a window open. Didn't matter, though. He'd come prepared with lock picking tools. Back when he'd been a teenager and interested in anything mechanical, he'd spent a couple of weeks practicing picking locks, a skill that had come in handy more than once over the years.

He approached the cabin cautiously, verified the place was still empty, then checked the doors. No luck. Returning to the back door, out of sight of anyone driving by, he extracted the little case with his tools, pulled on latex gloves, and got to work. Within minutes he'd defeated the handset and the deadbolt, and was inside. So much for the cop valuing security, the place didn't even have an alarm.

Moving through the kitchen, he sneered at the cramped space and unsophisticated appliances, but understood that common people made do with the simple and the banal. This mission was reconnaissance, to find out what he could about Murphy, and to search Meg's belongings for a flash drive or perhaps a portable hard drive. He'd also work out a plan for how to mete out the punishment they both deserved.

The most interesting thing of value in the living room was a laptop sitting amid piles of papers and books on a table. Not Meg's. Julius left it there while he continued his search. He could pick it up later if he decided taking it outweighed leaving evidence of a break-in. Movement on the couch had his heart stopping, but it was only a filthy cat, darting away to hide under a chair. Great, now his allergies would start up. He paused at the front window to verify the driveway remained clear, then took the stairs to the top floor.

That he found Meg's belongings in a tiny bedroom didn't fool him into thinking she was sleeping alone, because he also found condom wrappers in the bathroom trashcan. Sex was such a messy business. Long ago he'd given up engaging women for the purposes of sex. With diseases and the threat of an unwanted pregnancy, it was too risky all around.

He knew without a doubt that some woman would find carrying his child the perfect tool to extort money from him. He'd found self-pleasuring while watching porn much more satisfactory, though he rarely bothered anymore. At some point he'd father a son because the world needed the smartest people to procreate, to be the leaders and innovators of the next generation. God knew the lesser sort were multiplying at an alarming rate. He'd given quite a bit of thought to the idea of allowing Meg to be the mother of his child, but now congratulated himself on the intuition that had stopped him from pursuing that avenue.

He let out a string of sneezes as he searched through her bag, cursing the cat as he wiped his watering eyes. Side pockets revealed nothing of importance. He tossed out clothing and toiletries until, bingo, he found her laptop at the bottom. But no data storage device. There was no time to go through the computer now, so coming to a decision, he grabbed it along with the power cord. A sense of urgency had him hurrying down the stairs. He gathered up the laptop from the table, wishing he'd thought to bring something to carry them in. He sneezed again, then left through the back door, not bothering to shut it behind him.

Chapter Twelve

The men stood up from the conference table as if ready to go to the cabin without delay.

"Wait." Meg looked at Brenda, then at the chief. "You're not arresting me?"

Brad shook his head. "I'll be in touch with the Santa Cruz PD and their district attorney to decide what they want to do. I don't think you pose a risk to the public, but rather had reason to fear for your own safety. My recommendation is you stick close to this guy," he indicated Declan. "You'll be safe with him. Now, let's take a drive to your cabin and look for that tracking device." Brad turned to Brenda, "Ms. Nguyen." He nodded before leaving the room.

Meg took a few minutes to confer with Brenda in private. The lawyer felt confident that Brad's concern for Meg's safety would color the way he'd share the case with the Santa Cruz PD. Brenda intended to contact an attorney friend who lived and worked in Santa Cruz to get some inside info on the DA down there. Meg thanked Brenda and they left the building together to find Declan waiting beside his SUV. Brenda waved at Declan before walking away in the direction of her office.

Meg sat beside Declan in the 4Runner as they drove back toward the cabin, and she had to admit to feeling an anticlimax. Despite his assurances to the contrary, she'd been sure she'd be behind bars by now.

"You going to admit I was right?"

"Is that important to you?"

"You bet." He grinned. "Go on, admit it."

"Okay, you were right. I'm not going to jail. Yet," she added.

"Why aren't you relieved?"

"I'm relieved I'm not sitting in a jail cell, but I still feel like there's a big rock looming over my head waiting for the smallest earthquake to bring it crashing down."

He gave her a sidelong glance. "One thing at a time, Meg. Trust me."

She wondered at his suddenly serious expression and sensed there was more to his words than what was on the surface.

"Look, I trust you, but it's not up to you to keep me safe, regardless of what Chief Gallagher thinks. I was raised to take care of myself."

His gaze was hot when it turned on her. "Jesus Christ, Meg. We all have different skill sets. Mine happens to be in dealing with people a hell of a lot more violent and dangerous than the asshole Merritt. Brad wasn't disrespecting you or the power of women when he said you can trust me to protect you."

She looked down at her hands. "I'm sorry. You're right, but I don't like being dependent on people. I'm used to taking care of myself."

"Sometimes you have to give a little."

"Yeah."

They turned into the cabin's driveway. The rain had stopped, but the wind now blew hard enough to make the tops of the tall pines surrounding the property sway. More snow had melted so the muddy patches were bigger than the remaining areas of snow. Declan pulled up to his usual spot in the back and they got out. The big SUV with a police department insignia on the door pulled up and parked beside her car.

A movement, a quick blur of motion by the shed, caught Meg's eye, and she made a detour as Declan went to join Brad. Not sure what she'd seen, she approached carefully. Maybe deer, like they'd seen on the road, had come down to the cabin. She peered around the corner to find nothing but the gently rising slope dotted with pine trees and a few clusters of boulders.

The wind grew stronger, making a roaring sound as it moved through the forest. A clatter from the back of the cabin had her looking for the source. Her stomach dropped. The wood-framed screen over the back door to the kitchen swung in the wind, and the door itself sat wide open. She ran to the cabin, calling for Declan. Her one thought was Buttercup.

If the private investigator, or perhaps Julius, had broken into the cabin, the little cat could be in danger, or might have run out to be lost in the woods. Meg skidded to a stop, forcing herself to think before racing into the cabin. Buttercup may be in danger, but Meg charging inside when there might be an intruder wasn't going to help her.

Pounding feet sounded and the two men rounded the side of the cabin. The expression on Declan's face had her heart hammering. He reached her first, gripping her arms, fingers biting through her jacket.

"What is it?"

"Dex, you armed?" Brad interrupted, his voice utterly calm.

Declan's head snapped around, and Meg could see the cop persona settle on him like a well-fitting suit of armor. Brad had his radio off his belt, calling for backup.

Declan pulled his keys and cell phone out of his pocket and shoved them in Meg's hands. "Go lock yourself in my truck. If someone comes out of the cabin that's not me or Brad, get the hell out of here."

"What about Buttercup? I want to look for her out here in case she got out."

"I don't have time to argue. Do what I said. Now."

Backing toward the 4Runner, she watched Declan reach down to pull up a pant leg and retrieve a gun from a holster strapped to his shin. Brad already stood by the door, weapon in hand. He nodded to Declan, and they both disappeared inside.

Hating that she was of no use, but smart enough to realize both men would be safer if she did what Declan asked, she opened the door to the truck and locked herself in. Where earlier time seemed to scream by at lightning speed, now the seconds crawled by at a sluggish pace. The kitchen door was now closed, and she could see nothing through the few windows that faced out the back of the cabin. Her thumbnail was chewed down to the quick by the time the door opened again and Declan emerged, tucking his gun into the back waistband of his jeans with one hand as he held a bundle in front of him with his other.

She was out of the truck and running toward him before she had formed the thought to move. She drew near and saw the bundle was Buttercup cradled in his arms. Meg's heart gave a serious lurch. She didn't know if she had ever seen a man more sexy and wonderful than this one who had brought the little cat out to ease her worry.

"Buttercup is okay," she mumbled, struggling to keep her voice steady.

"Yeah, she is. Good thing, or I'd have to answer to my niece, and she's scary."

She thought he was intentionally trying to lighten her mood. "You love this cat, too."

"Maybe." He gave her the cat. Then his voice deepened. "He's been here, gone through our stuff."

"Who? Julius?" The joy at seeing the cat safe dimmed at Declan's announcement. She'd felt secure at the cabin, and now that sanctuary had been violated.

"Pretty sure. He took my laptop, and I think yours, too." His words were clipped, his body tense, and she could all but see the anger bubbling beneath the surface.

"Oh no. I'm so sorry, Declan, your book."

"I back it up to my cloud account at least once a day, so I won't have lost much there. Where were you keeping your laptop?"

"I'd packed it at the bottom of my black bag this morning."

"Then he has yours, too."

Brad trotted around from the front. "I think he must have come in on foot. The only tire tracks are yours and mine. Let's start walking a perimeter to see if we can pick up his trail. Should be easy to see in all this mud and snow."

"Let me put Buttercup in the house, then I'll help."

Declan nodded. Brad had a radio in his hand and was giving orders for responding units to check houses in the neighborhood for anything unusual.

Meg took the cat into the cabin, made sure both doors were shut, and went out again to join Declan. They started close to the cabin, then spread out in a circular fashion, until Declan called out, "I've got tracks here, going up behind the shed."

"Oh. That must have been him I saw earlier."

"You saw him? Why didn't you say anything?"

Brad joined them, head bent as he listened.

"When we first got here, I thought I saw something move behind the shed. You went toward the front where Brad was, so I went to see. I thought maybe it could be deer."

He scrubbed a hand over his face. "Damn it. Okay, did you see anything else?"

"That's it. If it had been him, he could have been hiding behind a tree or those boulders or something."

He gave a curt nod, then the three of them continued up the slope, the trail so obvious that even untrained, Meg could easily follow it. She didn't know how she'd missed it earlier. Spotting something on the ground, she reached down, only to have Brad calling to her. "Wait. Don't pick up anything you find. We'll want to preserve any prints."

"Here's a computer charging cord. I think it's Declan's."

The men moved swiftly, their heavy boots making squishing sounds on the moist earth. Using a twig, Declan picked up the cable and Brad opened an evidence bag for him to drop the cord into.

"Fucking bastard," Declan muttered. He frowned as he looked at Meg. "Is your laptop password protected?"

"Yes. Is yours?"

"Yeah. That will slow him down at least."

They continued following the footprints through the soft earth, now heading down the slope to the neighboring house south of the cabin. They found a single nitrile glove, which also went into an evidence bag. The sound of a car engine roaring to life reached them over the rising wind. Declan broke into a run while Brad got on his radio.

When Meg arrived at the neighboring cabin with Brad, Declan stood in front, shaking his head. "He was gone before I could see anything." He directed his question at Meg, "What kind of car does Merritt drive?"

"He has several. A Tesla, Lotus Elise, and a Mercedes. There are others, but I don't remember all of them. He likes cars."

Brad contacted his department dispatcher to communicate with other units to be on the lookout for any of those vehicles. Examination of the driveway showed tracks, but no evidence anyone had entered the home.

"Damn, we just missed him."

***

Dex shoved his phone in his pocket and stood on the porch as the evening sky turned to dusk, hoping to calm the buzzing in his brain. The last police vehicle disappeared down the driveway, brake lights glowing red. The FBI had confirmed that the private investigator had indeed been hired by Julius Merritt and was currently in Sacramento. Merritt had been spotted leaving his home in Santa Cruz early that morning, so he'd had enough time to get to Hangman's Loss. And now he'd been able to slip past officers canvassing the area. Who knew where he was hiding out.

An officer had come in with a forensics kit to dust for prints. Given the glove they'd recovered, Dex was sure she hadn't found anything inside the cabin, but the glove might prove fruitful. He'd seen more than one idiot discard a glove after a crime, not realizing their fingerprint might be perfectly preserved inside the latex.

The call with his contact at the FBI had Dex wanting to slam a fist through a wall. Throughout his career he'd had plenty of contact with the FBI so he knew not all agents were assholes, but this guy certainly qualified. Dex understood why Special Agent Esteban Delgado wanted him to follow the course of action he'd laid out weeks ago, but that didn't mean Dex agreed that it was the best plan, especially now that it meant continuing to deceive Meg, and that pissed him off.

When she had spilled about her relationship with Merritt, he'd kept quiet about his own past with the bastard. What were the odds of Merritt's involvement with the woman who'd showed up on his doorstep? As soon as he realized who she was running from, he'd put in a call to his contact at the Bureau.

A few months ago, Delgado had approached him about the possibility of Dex working with the FBI to bring in Merritt. Beyond the issues with the compromised medical devices, which the FBI was already investigating, Merritt was suspected of being at the center of a web of "accidents," computer hacks, and physical attacks that had left dozens of lives ruined.

The feds needed proof, and given Dex's past with the asshole, they had recruited Dex to try to lure the fucker into acting. Their reasoning was based on their belief that Merritt had a pattern of seeking retribution against anyone who crossed him, and if they could turn his attention to Dex, Merritt would try to go after him and they could catch Merritt in the act. Given that his arrest all those years ago had let the public see him as the spoiled man-child he was, the FBI probably wasn't wrong.

Now that Delgado knew of Meg's involvement with Merritt, the FBI saw the case taking a different direction. Since Merritt knew from his PI that there was a connection between Meg and Dex, the temptation to seek revenge against them both would be too much to resist. Today's break-in was evidence of the presumption that the fucker would come after them himself to mete out consequences more severe than if he delegated the reprisal to an underling.

But the FBI didn't want Meg to know any of it—the case they were building, and Dex's involvement with the investigation. They didn't want there to be any chance she'd tip off Merritt. Dex had argued the stupidity of that assertion since her life was in danger. But the fucking feds insisted that since she was an untrained civilian, she could end up being a liability if she knew too much.

Dex had told them he'd drop out of the whole deal unless they promised they wouldn't pursue federal charges against Meg, and that any potential danger to her would be mitigated. He hated making decisions for her, and he'd bet his left nut she'd be furious with him when she found out, but he didn't see any way around it. He wanted Merritt to go down, and if he stayed on the case, he'd have control over the situation and, most importantly, Meg's safety.

Throw their burgeoning relationship into the mix and this was a mess no matter how Dex sliced it. Sex with Meg might have been a mistake, but he didn't regret it. He worried though if he was being fair to her. *I don't want to fall in love with you.* Those words had hit him like a punch to the heart. He'd fucked up with his wife, not that he'd managed that all on his own.

This woman drew out all his protective instincts, but he wondered if he should really be guarding his own heart.

Reentering the cabin, Dex noted Meg had been busy. Fingerprint powder was messy, and she'd cleaned the surfaces the officer had dusted for prints. He found her in the kitchen, staring into the refrigerator.

He reached past her to snag a longneck bottle of beer. "Hungry?"

She seemed preoccupied, and there were shadows in her eyes when she looked up at him. He had to block the impulse to smooth back her hair, kiss her forehead, fold her into a hug. The night before had been intense, both emotionally and physically, at least for him.

But she wasn't giving much away. He didn't know if the coming night would end up with her back in his bed. He damn well hoped so, but the next move would have to come from her.

She gave him a searching look before answering his question. "We missed lunch, and there's nothing in here to make into dinner. I can run into town to pick up groceries. I don't think it matters anymore if I use my credit card. Julius knows where I am."

He set the unopened beer back in the fridge. "We'll eat out."

She shut the refrigerator door. "Where?"

"Your choice. I haven't gone out much since I got here. Word is the Brew Pub is good. Maddy says they have amazing onion rings, if that does anything for you. Their craft brew is worthy." He thought for a minute. "There's also a pizza place on Main that opened recently." He shrugged. "I'm sure there are other restaurants, but we'd have to drive around to see what."

"We had pizza, so why don't we go to the Brew Pub? I'd be willing to try the onion rings."

In minutes, they were in the 4Runner and on their way into town. Meg hadn't taken forever to get ready, which he appreciated. That might have more to do with the fact that she didn't have any makeup in her bags than her lack of fussiness, but he'd take it as a win.

He also liked that she hadn't made a big deal about picking a place to eat. His ex-wife used to all the time. When he'd been married, going out had never been straightforward. If he'd asked Megan where she wanted to go, she'd ask where *he* wanted to go. If he picked a place and said let's go here, she'd complain because she hadn't really wanted to go there. If he suggested someplace new, it took thirty minutes of consulting Yelp reviews, which he figured were bogus anyway, for her to decide. He'd never been able to figure out the perfect formula that would get them out of the house and to a restaurant they'd both be happy with without all the damned hassle.

Dex opened the door to Hangman's Brew Pub, letting Meg precede him. The place was seat-yourself and not crowded, though a group at the bar jeered loudly at a game on the TV. He pointed to an empty booth. Framed photos of Hangman's Loss's Wild West days decorated the walls, and hanging pendant lights gave each table an intimate feel. Two women were seated in a booth behind the one Declan was aiming for, and they both smiled broadly as they approached.

"Declan, it's good to see you." The striking woman with the razor-sharp cheekbones rose from her seat to engulf him in a hug. It never failed to surprise him that the friends he'd made in Hangman's Loss accepted him without reservation and treated him like family. Helping to find Maddy when she'd been kidnapped had apparently been the cement to those relationships.

"Meghan, this is Dory Calderon."

Dory's smile was friendly. "Hi, Meghan."

The other woman seated at the table rose and pressed a kiss to Declan's cheek.

"And this is Emma Gallagher, Brad's wife."

"Nice to meet you, Meg. Brad told me about you," Emma said. "I'm glad you've come to Hangman's Loss. There are good people here who all want you to be safe."

"Thank you. I like your husband. He's steady and fair."

"Brad's the best," Dory spoke up. "He was a rock when I was having trouble with my ex-husband."

"How did you ladies score a girls' night out?" Dex asked.

Dory flashed a wide smile. "Grandparents are awesome. Adrian is baking cookies with my parents tonight, and little Owen is with his grandma since his daddy is on duty."

A knot of young men at the bar let out a screaming yell. They were watching the mega TV screen where tall athletes were fighting over a basketball. Declan had never found games played by millionaires entertaining, but the group of twenty-somethings did, and were loud about it. He judged they were well on their way to being lit. Hopefully the bartender would be willing to cut them off.

A few other patrons sat around the dining area and looked like they were mostly trying to ignore the idiots.

Dory slid back into her seat, and before Emma did the same, she leaned toward him. "I called Brad and he's on his way. Deb can handle those guys, but she shouldn't have to."

"Deb the bartender?"

"Yeah. She's working every extra shift she can pick up to pay for her son to go through rehab, and she shouldn't have to deal with obnoxious drunks."

Dex nodded. "I'll keep an eye on them until Brad gets here."

He took the far seat in the booth so he would have a clear view of the bar. Meg sat across from him, and studied the menu with great concentration, her expression serious. When she glanced up, she caught him looking and blushed slightly, then pointed to an item on the menu. "Do you want to split an order of onion rings? It says here they come with three different dipping sauces."

"Sure." He figured he couldn't spend the whole evening simply looking at her, so he'd better put some effort into conversation. "What else do you want?"

"I think a veggie burger."

"Why veggie? You're not vegetarian."

"You're right, I'm not, but I don't like big hunks of meat, either. What are you having?"

"A big hunk of meat."

That brought a smile and a dimple. The waiter took their orders with brisk efficiency, and when he left, Dex reached in his pocket to pull out a plastic bag. Inside was a small black box. He laid the bag on the table between them.

"What's that?"

"The GPS tracking device Merritt attached inside the rear passenger-side tire well of your car."

She picked up the bag, turned it so she could study the tracker. "The bastard."

"Exactly. He's known where you were all along."

"And probably has known everywhere I've gone since I started working for him." She pushed the bag back to him. "Is that illegal?"

"It's invasion of privacy." He put it back in his pocket. "Brad needs this back to document as evidence, but I wanted to show you."

"He knows we're right here, right now."

"No, I disconnected the battery so it's no longer sending a signal. But now he knows we found it."

"Aren't you worried that he could come back tonight? That he'll break into the cabin again? He could even break in when we're home."

He shook his head. Dory's bright laughter carried from the next table. "I don't think so. He could be escalating, but my take is he's a coward at heart. I think he's holed up someplace, maybe renting a cabin nearby. Or he could have gone back to Santa Cruz. He'll want time to get into our laptops."

"Wouldn't the police find and question him if he went back to his house?"

"We're not positive he's the one who broke in today. They couldn't get a print out of the glove we found, so right now, he's clear. They could get a warrant to search his place, but by the time that happens he'll have ditched the computers."

Meg picked up a paper napkin and began folding and unfolding it carefully. "I'm sorry," she muttered.

"For what?"

"For everything that happened today. Your home being broken into, your laptop stolen, Buttercup being frightened. For getting you involved in my messy business."

"What happened today was because of Merritt, not anything you did."

"That's not true. I know ultimately he's to blame, but I brought it on you. If I'd known Dad was letting someone use the cabin, I would never have come."

Dex drummed his fingers on the table. Merritt coming after him was about more than his relationship with Meg, but he couldn't tell her that even if it would ease her guilt. "Where would you have gone?"

She shrugged. "Doesn't matter now."

"There's another way to look at this, you know." What he wanted to say would lay it out in the open right at the time when being honest with her was forbidden. But suddenly he didn't give a shit. Meg pulled at something in him and for the first time in a long while, he thought he might have found someone who could ease the loneliness that plagued him. He didn't feel right starting a relationship with her when he hadn't been completely honest.

He leaned forward in his seat and reached across the table to pick up her hand. He set aside the folded napkin and rubbed his thumb against her palm. He liked that her nails were real. He'd had never gotten why women spent so much money to get the fake ones that looked like talons. He pressed his hand against hers, palm to palm. Her fingers were slender but strong, and barely reached past his middle knuckle. Her eyes were on him, and it gave him a kick to realize her respiration rate had increased. Nice to know he wasn't the only one stirred up.

The words to tell her about his relationship with Merritt stuck in his throat. Damn. Telling her meant breaking a promise. As much as he disliked Special Agent Delgado, Dex couldn't compromise the mission. But if he didn't say anything and Meg later found out he hadn't been honest, then he was equally fucked.

He laced his fingers with hers and brought their joined hands to his mouth where he brushed the back of her hand with his lips. At her questioning look, he held back on what he really wanted to say, instead murmuring, "Another time."

Chapter Thirteen

Meg wondered why she wasn't a puddle of lusty, greedy need melted onto the seat. When Declan focused his attention on her, she felt like the only woman in the world. He must emit pheromones that were extra potent, because he'd succeeded in not only distracting her from the events of the day, but also turned her into a hot mess.

And she really wanted to know what he'd been about to say when he'd been all but making love to her hand. If she wasn't so hungry, she'd suggest they ditch the restaurant and go straight back to the cabin and his big bed, which was next to the drawer that held the box of condoms. The guys at the bar yelled in unison, a welcome distraction, then jeered not-so-welcome profanities when an on-screen player was called on a foul. The waiter approached with their meal, casting a wary eye on the basketball fans. He arranged their plates on the table as another loud cry erupted.

"Bartender good about cutting them off?" Declan asked.

"Usually," the young man replied. "But we're short-staffed tonight, and they look like the belligerent type."

Meg surveyed the group. There were five young men who looked seriously unhappy with the progress of the game. She was glad she'd totally missed the stage in life where getting drunk and obnoxious in public was a thing to do.

"Cops have been called, but I'll help if needed before then."

The waiter thanked Declan, then hustled to service his other tables.

The huge platter of onion rings smelled amazing. Meg picked one up, dunked it in the dip that looked like ranch, and took a bite—and was immediately transported to heaven. "Oh my god. These are amazing."

Declan dipped an onion ring in a different sauce, then crunched down and chased it with a pull on his beer. "Hmm, you're right. Fucking amazing."

Telling herself she couldn't shove all the onion rings in her face, Meg bit into her veggie burger. It was good, but didn't hit the same note as the onion rings.

One of the boys at the bar let out a whoop and shoved the friend next to him, who shoved back harder. Declan tensed, but the guys got distracted by the action on the court and settled down.

Despite the noisy young men, Meg enjoyed her meal, but more, she enjoyed the time with Declan. Swallowing a bite of burger, she asked him, "What is your goal as a writer?"

He shrugged. "Be successful."

"How do you define success?"

"Making enough money to live comfortably. I'm not drawing on my pension right now because it will pay better if I wait until I'm older. I want to be successful enough to support myself by writing." He paused. "What about you?"

"To do what I love, which is writing, and, like you, make a comfortable living from it, be able to travel some. I'd like to take my mom on a trip. She's always wanted to go to Ireland, and I want to take her. She sacrificed so much raising me, and I want to give her that."

The way his gaze warmed had her heart beating heavily.

The door to the pub opened, and the group at the bar quieted. Meg turned her head. Bradley Gallagher strode in, accompanied by a giant of a man. The big man wore a police uniform, and both wore sidearms and badges. Each gave the crowd at the bar that assessing cop look, the same one she'd seen in Declan's eyes when they'd walked in. Brad acknowledged Declan with a nod, while the big guy focused on the two women sitting in the next booth as they headed across the room.

Emma rose to greet her husband, going up on her tiptoes to deliver a sweet kiss. The officer's coat had "Capt. Morgan" stitched in yellow thread on the front. Meg would have to be blind to miss his quickly veiled expression as his gaze rested on Dory before he turned to Declan.

"Dex. Sorry to interrupt." He nodded to the group at the bar. "Think they'll settle down?"

Declan shrugged. "Maybe. They quieted once they saw you two. But they're dumb and drunk, so I doubt that's going to last." He made the introductions. "Meghan, this is Captain Jack Morgan."

Meg scooted over to make room. "Nice to meet you, have a seat."

Jack slid into the booth, and Meg didn't think she was imagining Declan's resigned expression. She liked his friends, but had been enjoying the two of them being alone.

Brad stepped over. "Sorry if we're crashing your date." He glanced from Declan to Meg. "You mind if I pull up a table so we can all sit together?"

"Of course not," she answered, at the same time Declan said, "Yes."

Their response didn't seem to matter, because Emma and Dory were already moving with their plates to the table Brad pushed up.

The waiter arrived and Brad ordered coffee, Jack waving his hand to pass.

"Ooh, the onion rings!" Dory snagged a crispy ring and dunked it in the ranch dip. "Maddy says they're orgasmic. She and Logan shared these when he was first back in town and look where they are now."

Jack's expression turned intense when Dory closed her eyes to savor the taste.

"Don't say 'orgasmic' and my sister's name in the same sentence unless you want me to be permanently scarred," Brad growled.

"Aww, sweetie, you didn't know your sister has sex?" Dory grinned.

"Stop it."

"Maybe you could tell yourself the twins are the product of an immaculate conception." Dory patted his hand.

"You're not much help."

Curious, Meg asked, "Tell me if I'm remembering Declan's story correctly. He said you and Emma own a business together?"

"Kind of," Emma replied, taking a sip from her wine. "I inherited the resort from my grandfather and Dory helped me get it up and running. About nine months ago, Dory came up with the idea of converting one area into a wedding or special event venue. She invested in the project, and that will be her business."

"And the catering will be done out of Maddy's café, with Eva doing the bulk of the jobs while the twins are small," Dory added.

"That sounds like fun, but a lot of work."

"It is. Once we're a little father along we'll be able to hire more help to ease the burden. But let's get back to you." Dory wagged her brows suggestively. "This guy treating you well?" She nodded her head toward Declan.

"Well, he hasn't taken me on an Italian vacation, but we did go snowshoeing."

"No Italian vacations? You're slacking, Dex," Dory teased.

"We were on a date, you know, *just* the two of us, when half the town showed up. Maybe I was going to ask her to go with me to Italy but you all spoiled the moment."

"Move too slow, dude, and you'll miss your shot," Jack muttered.

"What's that supposed to mean?" Dory's tone held a sharp edge, making Meg wonder at their history. Deep undercurrents didn't even begin to describe the tension between them.

Jack faced Dory squarely. "Exactly that, Isadora. No mystery."

Dory opened her mouth with what Meg was sure would be a sharp retort, when high-volume obscenities erupted from one of the guys at the bar as the basketball game wound down to the final seconds.

Brad sighed, eyeing Declan and Jack as he spoke. "The dumbasses haven't taken the opportunity to change the way they enjoy the game. I thought the police presence would be a deterrent. We'll need to clear them out before we leave."

"Yeah," Jack agreed. "Deb is good, but she shouldn't have to deal with the shit they're likely to heap on her."

A shout had all eyes pivoting to the scene at the bar. The chief obscenity yeller had stumbled into a table, and instead of righting himself, lurched unsteadily into the waiter. Both the waiter and the loaded tray he was carrying hit the ground and glasses shattered with a mighty crash.

The young man appeared to need a moment to process the scene, but then laughed loudly at the waiter still picking himself up off the floor. "Watch where you're going, asshole."

"That's it. You're done here." The bartender picked up a remote and turned off the TV.

"Turn it back on, bitch."

"Time's up." Brad stood up from the table. "You," he pointed to Declan, "are deputized."

"Ah, shit," Declan muttered, but rose to his feet.

"Excuse us," Brad said to the women. Meg watched, fascinated, as the scene unfolded. The police chief, the police captain, and the former LAPD detective stood shoulder to shoulder. They looked impressive in a way that said, "We don't take any bullshit." The young men were about to have their asses handed to them.

Brad held out his badge, identifying himself as chief of police.

"You gentlemen are drunk," he addressed them, "and well on your way to disorderly. You've got two choices. One, after you clean up the mess you made and pay for the breakage," he indicated the broken glass and overturned table, "you get out your phones and call your mommies or girlfriends and get them to come pick up your sorry asses because, news flash, not one of you is getting behind the wheel tonight."

"What's option two, dumbshit?" This came from the guy who had caused the mishap.

"Option two, you don't pick option one and I haul your asses to jail and you stay there until morning when I have the time to sort out charges. I guess there's now an option three where you call me dumbshit again, and I haul you in regardless and see what other charges I can add."

One of the guy's buddies grabbed his arm. "C'mon, Trent. Look at these dudes, they're seriously badass. I don't want to get into it with them."

Trent shook him off, shoving away and moving toward Brad. Declan and Jack stepped forward, but Brad put up a hand to stop them. He pointed at the other young men who were looking increasingly uncertain. "Get your phones out and make those calls. Now, or I see how fast these two," he indicated Jack and Declan, "can have you on your asses and Mirandized. You can come back in the morning for your cars. You don't need to compound your shit because Trent here hasn't figured out how to pull his head out."

Trent looked for backup but the guys already had their phones out. "You're a bunch of wusses," he whined. Without the support of his friends, he seemed to deflate—head hanging, shoulders slumping. He reminded Meg of a recalcitrant child being told it was time for bed. He reached down to right the table. Deb the bartender, who looked tough enough to have taken them on her own, brought out a broom and dustpan to hand to him.

"Thanks for the assist, Brad." She turned to Trent, who began to halfheartedly sweep up glass. "Here's a lesson," she told him. "No one likes a mean drunk, and that's what you are. This is the second time you've behaved this way in my bar. If you come in here and act like an idiot again, you won't be allowed back."

With the situation under control the men returned to the table, but this time Declan slid into the seat next to Meg, leaving the others to occupy the bench across from them and the added seats.

Brad had handled the guys at the bar with a minimum of fuss, and she couldn't deny thinking Declan looked damned sexy as backup. They picked up the conversation with easy familiarity, going over the events of the day. Spending time with the friendly group made her wonder what it would be like to live in Hangman's Loss and be part of this community full-time. Maybe she would find her place with the circle of women that included Emma, Dory, and Maddy.

Throughout the conversation, Declan drummed his fingers on the table and tapped his foot, restlessly shifting in his seat. She cast a glance at him to see why he was so antsy. The hot look he shot back gave her the answer.

She stifled a grin at his barely concealed sigh when Emma began a story of her son Owen's efforts to get their dog to obey him. She pulled up a video on her phone showing the toddler shaking a finger at the dog and yelling "No" with impressive volume.

"The kid's first word was no. Can you believe it?" The proud-daddy tone came through in Brad's voice.

"Adrian's first word was 'my,'" Dory said. "At first I thought he was trying to say 'ma,' as he should have, but I learned pretty fast my was short for mine."

Meg didn't think the others heard Declan's frustrated groan, but a moment later he grabbed her hand and rose from the table, bringing Meg with him. Tossing a fistful of twenties on the table, he said, "Sorry to break up the party, but we're out of here."

Dory sent her a knowing grin that had a warm flush heating Meg's cheeks.

She could hardly say her own good-byes before Declan was escorting her out the door. "In a hurry much?" she asked.

He didn't say anything, pulling her across the darkened parking lot to where the 4Runner sat in the glow cast by a light pole. The clouds that might have kept the temperatures above freezing had cleared out, and now a silvery moon hung in a bitterly cold sky, making Meg wish she had a heavier coat. A vehicle started a few rows over, its headlights shining brightly in her eyes before it sped away.

Declan backed Meg against the passenger door of the truck, leaned in, and took her lips in a fiery kiss that about singed her hair, making the cold temperature a moot issue. She ran her fingers through his beard when his lips left hers to dip into the hollow of her throat. He pushed open her jacket and trailed a line of kisses across her shoulder, edging toward the upward slope of her breast.

"Oh my god, Declan." The words came out on a wheezy moan. With him having played with her hands earlier, now he'd revved her engines from a low idle to full throttle in about ten seconds flat. He stepped back, lifting his hands carefully as if he thought she might spin completely out of control. Or maybe he'd be the one spinning out.

"Sorry," he mumbled. He took another step back, scrubbing a big hand over his face, his beard making a quiet crinkling sound. "Lost control there."

"Hmm. I like it when you lose control." She took a step toward him, reaching to hook a finger in his belt and pull him closer. She eyed the bulge straining against the material of his pants and grinned up at him, making sure to press right there when she pulled him against her. This time she initiated the lip touch, and by the end of the hot, wet, consuming kiss, she wanted to climb him like a tree. She tugged his head down, nipped his earlobe, and whispered, "Why don't we head home where we can lose control in a not-quite-so-public place?"

"Praise Jesus, yes." He was already circling the hood of the 4Runner. "Let's go."

Meg reached for the door handle, then paused. "Ah, Declan, a little problem has arisen."

"It's not so little, sweetheart."

"Ha. No, I wasn't talking about what you keep in your pants." She pointed as he returned to her side of the vehicle. "I'm talking about the seriously mutilated tire you have here."

His string of profanity was long and inventive. The tire wasn't simply flat. It had been hacked at to the point the rubber hung off it in shreds. Declan whipped his head around, doing a quick scan of the parking lot. Two of the young men from the bar stood near the door of the pub, likely waiting for their rides, and weren't paying them any attention. There was no one else in the parking lot.

Declan tugged out his phone, tapped the screen, and spoke a few brief words, then used it to take pictures of the tire from several angles. Within seconds, Brad and Jack joined them.

"Son of a bitch," Brad swore softly as he studied the tire.

Jack loped off across the lot, doing a quick survey of the vehicles parked there. He returned a minute later, shaking his head at Brad's questioning look. "No one else was hit."

"Seems to me it takes a lot of rage to mutilate a tire like that," Meg said. She wrapped her arms around herself, suddenly cold. "I think Declan was targeted. It could have been Julius, this is the kind of childish payback he'd engage in."

"Or it could have been one of the drunks," muttered Jack. "But you'd think they'd go after the police cruiser. And if someone really wanted to be an asshole, they'd get all four tires."

"The asshole may have been interrupted. A car two rows over started up and took off when we got out here."

"You get make or model?" Brad asked. "We can put out a BOLO."

"No."

Meg glanced up at Declan's curt reply. They'd been too wrapped up in each other for either one of them to notice.

Declan pulled open the back of the 4Runner, motions jerky. He set the jack and a lug wrench on the ground next to the shredded tire. He pulled off his coat and draped it around her shoulders, engulfing her in warmth and his scent. Then he scooted under the rear end where Meg assumed the spare was. While Brad spoke into his phone, Jack helped Declan and they quickly swapped tires. Declan threw the damaged tire into the back of the vehicle and retrieved a rag to wipe the dirt from his hands.

Brad shoved his phone in his pocket. "Gustavo's Tires out near the highway will take good care of you when you want to replace the tire." At Declan's curt nod, Brad continued, "I'll do the police report. You can come in tomorrow to look it over if you want to go on home now."

***

Meg sat in the passenger seat as Declan drove the winding road back to the cabin, the full moon and tall pines casting alternating patterns of light and shadow across the windshield. The moments of intense desire had vanished like a puff of vapor into the cold night air, and Meg pulled Declan's coat tighter around her as she suppressed a shiver.

He stopped in front of the cabin and sat motionless, hands gripping the steering wheel. Meg would be the first to admit she didn't have a lot of experience with men's moods, but she'd take a guess that Declan was still angry. She opened the car door and stepped out, waiting on the porch until he joined her. He unlocked the door, and when she would have stepped inside, he lay a hand on her arm to hold her back.

"Wait out here. I want to make sure we haven't had another break-in."

She nodded, then gave a start of surprise when he bent down to retrieve the gun from a holster strapped to his shin. He slipped inside the house, flipping on lights as he went, and was back minutes later.

"We're clear," he told her as he bent to return his gun to the holster.

She shut the door and would have walked past him if he hadn't snagged her wrist. "Meghan."

Her heart gave that traitorous thud as she turned to face him. His serious expression was back, and she gave into the impulse and reached out a forefinger to rub the crease between his brows. "You've got your broody face on."

He caught her hand in his and brought it to his lips. "Broody face? I think you mean pissed-off face."

"I'm sorry about your tire."

"It's not only the tire. I don't like someone fucking with me. Merritt broke in here today, then he slashed my tire this evening. That seriously pisses me off."

"You don't think it was one of those boys at the bar?"

"No. If they were going to go after anyone, they would have hit Brad's official-looking police vehicle. They couldn't have known which car was mine."

"Right."

He let go of her hands to lay his on her hips and pull her against him. "Nothing like a slashed tire to kill the mood."

"Hmm," she murmured as she leaned forward to press her lips to the intriguing skin between his beard and collar. "I don't think the mood is all the way dead."

Chapter Fourteen

Julius cursed when the big car slid on the icy road. He spun the wheel and the high beams reflected against a guardrail unnervingly close, and rocks scraped against the undercarriage. The car lurched to a stop and he drew in a shuddering breath. The moonlight didn't penetrate beyond the barrier and he could only guess that he was inches from the edge of a cliff. Carefully steering back onto the highway, for the first time he questioned his decision to drive back to Santa Cruz that night.

Attacking the asshole Murphy's tire had been strangely cathartic. His only regret was that he hadn't been able to give all the tires the same treatment. There'd been that jolt of fear when the door of the bar had swung open and Murphy and Meg had walked through. He'd barely had time to get to his car, and since he wasn't sure they hadn't seen him, he'd thought it prudent to leave town. Even now he had to force himself to hold down his speed on the curving mountain road. Why the hell weren't there fucking streetlights? The night's murky blackness felt oppressive, the road stretching endlessly ahead of him.

In approximately three hours he'd be back in Santa Cruz. He'd catch a few hours' sleep, then he'd get his tech guy to break into the computers Julius had swiped from the cabin. Now, he was more certain than ever that Meg had been planted in his home at Murphy's direction, and that the ex-cop had some plot to destroy all that Julius had built. But Julius was smarter than either of them, and he needed only a bit more time to work out the details to a plan for retribution, a plan that would give the bastard Murphy what he deserved. The satisfaction of slashing the asshole's tires would be nothing compared to how Julius would feel when he finally, *finally,* brought down the man who had humiliated him all those years ago.

Meg Bennett would also be punished with the same act of justice, a scenario that appealed to Julius's sense of efficiency.

He considered his options. Humiliating Murphy held particular appeal, and the idea of how to do that had come to him when he'd swiped the laptop. He needed time to implement that plan. He ran through possibilities for Meg that would enhance the feeling of justice. She was close to her mother, so maybe arranging a little accident for the parent would work as a precursor to the final event. He'd make sure Meg knew her mother had suffered because of the daughter's actions.

Julius was good at causing *accidents* without leaving a trace of evidence. The entire campaign would climax with the deaths of both Murphy and Meg. His plan hadn't originally been to murder them. He didn't even like putting it in those terms. But he'd come to the inescapable conclusion that the scales of justice wouldn't be appropriately balanced until both were dead.

***

Meg rolled onto her side and opened her eyes to the half-light of early morning, not surprised to find herself at the outer edge of the mattress. She poked muscled ribs to prod Declan to move over. Buttercup stood from her spot at the foot of the bed, stretched, and hopped down to pad quietly to the door. Declan shifted but in the wrong direction and pushed her perilously close to falling out of bed.

She poked him again, and let out a startled squeak when he wrapped an arm around her and rolled until she lay on her back, his solid body over her. Her startled gasp morphed into a sigh when his lips closed over hers. Her hands journeyed down until they found his erection, and now it was his turn to sigh while she stroked and caressed. The way he watched her from those sleepy eyes, as if he were paying attention to every nuance of her response, as if her experience was so much more important than his own, had her wishing they had met under different circumstances.

He pushed aside his t-shirt she was wearing and dipped his head to trail his lips first to one breast, then the other, nipping and teasing, then drifted lower across her belly, then lower still. Declan's intense focus on her pleasure had an orgasm overtaking her like a long roll of thunder, leaving her gasping in its wake. There was the crinkling of a foil wrapper, then he was there, deliciously hard, nudging her legs apart and moving forcefully into her. Meg had never been a double orgasm kind of girl, but Declan held himself back as once again he played her body like an instrument, building the desire, using his body to push both of them over the final edge.

When he sprawled over her, his thundering heart hammering against her own, the realization dawned for Meg that she was exactly where she wanted to be. Maybe she wasn't ready to identify her emotions, but she understood herself enough to know that if she wasn't in love already, she was teetering on the brink.

If she'd met Declan without danger dogging her every step and the threat of prison hovering over the horizon, she wouldn't have had to work so hard on not falling in love with him. Keeping that distance was getting harder and harder to maintain, especially at moments like this.

Declan pulled the blankets up to her shoulders before rising out of bed for a quick trip to the bathroom. He returned and pulled Meg against his side. She didn't know how he could simply drift back to sleep, but that's exactly what he did with her hand resting on his chest as his breathing deepened. She allowed herself a few minutes to absorb the moment, wishing it could be more, then slipped quietly from his bed.

After a quick shower she headed for the kitchen. Once the coffee was brewing, she set about making the kind of Sunday morning breakfast her father had made for her with the same appliances.

She was pulling a tray of biscuits from the oven when Declan walked in with bare feet, wearing flannel pants and a thermal shirt, looking wonderfully rumpled. He made his way to the stove as she set the hot baking tray on a breadboard. "Is this sausage gravy? Are we having biscuits and sausage gravy?"

"Yes it is, and we are."

"Hot damn." He loosened a steaming biscuit from the tray and tossed it between his hands. When it had cooled enough, he broke off a corner and popped it in his mouth. After swallowing, he asked, "Did I mention you're incredible? I think it's been a decade since I've had made-from-scratch biscuits. These are amazing."

"They'd be even better if they were made with buttermilk, but in the absence of buttermilk, I had to make do."

Meg tried not to let his appreciation affect her, but it was hard. Everything about him was appealing. How he projected a gruff demeanor that couldn't hide his innate kindness. His unabashed enthusiasm for the food she prepared. And most of all, the way he acted when they were out together, as if he was in a room with a hundred other women, and he would see only her.

They sat down to breakfast, pale sunlight coming through the window. Buttercup lay curled on the chair next to Meg, busily licking her paw and rubbing it over her ears. They ate, shared the pot of coffee, and talked easily, in part because they both avoided mentioning the danger waiting in the wings.

If she were the dreaming type, she'd dream of this being one of many mornings like this. The yearning grabbed her by the throat and she knew she was heading for heartache.

***

Dex ran the water until it turned hot and began filling the dish basin. It felt right sharing breakfast with Meg. Even washing dishes wasn't bad when she stood with him at the sink ready to dry. He thought any situation would be better if she was with him. Hell, he was in deep, and he knew it. He found himself talking to her about personal things, things he never shared with anybody, but he'd also discovered that he could enjoy the silences with her as well. Spending time with someone who didn't feel compelled to fill every waking moment with chatter was soothing.

He rinsed the skillet and set it on the drainer, the chime of an incoming text pulling him out of the cozy world where it was only him and Meg. He wished cell phones had never been invented. He glanced at his phone. Delgado's text read, "Call me." Earlier, Dex had messaged the FBI agent to let him know about the shredded tire. No doubt Delgado would reach the same conclusion Dex and Brad had—Merritt was the most likely suspect.

With Meg curled on the couch with the cat on her lap and a novel she'd pulled from the bookshelf upstairs, he stepped outside. "What's up?" he asked when the call to Delgado connected.

"I'm on my way to that Podunk little town of yours. What the hell ever made you leave civilization? Is there even a Starbucks there?" Esteban Delgado's voice held no detectable regional accent.

He didn't sound old or young, and his voice wasn't particularly deep or high-pitched. Since Dex had never met him in person, he was speculating, but he'd bet the guy wore a suit even on his days off and shined his badge every morning when he got out of bed.

"I wanted to get away from annoying FBI agents."

"Easy, son. This FBI agent is going to be on your doorstep in about an hour. I want to talk to Meghan Bennett."

"What the hell for?" He knew he sounded pissed, but he didn't give a damn. Delgado was ruining a perfectly good morning.

"License plate reader picked up a vehicle owned by our boy Merritt in a little town north of you about nine-thirty last night. I just got off the phone with your town sheriff. He's not liking that we're taking over the investigation of the break-in at your place and the vandalism to your vehicle, but he's going to have to suck it up."

"That's police chief, not sheriff. And you're going to want to dial back the swagger, because Brad Gallagher is a smart man and you don't want to alienate him by being a prick."

Delgado's huffed-out breath came through loud and clear over the phone. "Anyone ever tell you your attitude sucks, Murphy?"

"Plenty of times. You still haven't told me why you want to talk to Meghan."

"I'll explain when I get there. You haven't told her about your history with Merritt, have you?"

"No."

"Good. It's better not to for the time being. The less she knows, the less she can divulge."

"Divulge to who? What are you planning, Delgado?"

"You'll find out when I get there."

Dex shoved his phone in his pocket, a sinking feeling in the pit of his stomach. Delgado wanted something from Meg, and Dex was positive he wasn't going to like it.

***

At the Hangman's Loss police station, Dex sat across the conference table from Special Agent Esteban Delgado. Brad Gallagher was at the end of the table between the two men. Dex had left Meghan back at the cabin, telling her he was getting together with Brad and Logan. He hadn't lied, but deliberately misleading her wasn't much better on the honesty scale. He wasn't happy with the situation, but he didn't trust Delgado to have her best interests at heart, so he wanted to hear what the FBI agent had to say before including her.

As expected, Delgado wore a gray suit like a uniform, his tie knotted snugly at his throat and his FBI badge hanging from his neck where no one could possibly miss it. The door opened once more, and Logan Ross entered carrying a steaming to-go cup with the logo of the café his wife owned.

Delgado looked askance at the former FBI agent as Logan took a seat at the end of the table.

"Ross, why are you in on this meeting? You're no longer FBI. I heard you're a beat cop now. That's quite a fall."

"Bite me. I'm here because Declan and Chief Gallagher want me here." Logan didn't bother commenting on the snide "beat cop" remark.

With his brows pulled down in an irritated scowl, Delgado took charge. "Gentlemen, this meeting is a courtesy to inform the local law enforcement agency of the ongoing investigation involving Julius Merritt, and now Meghan Bennett. The FBI will be taking over the investigation surrounding the break-in and robbery at the cabin where Declan Murphy is residing, as well as the vandalism to his vehicle that took place last evening. It is part of a larger case involving Merritt with which Murphy has been assisting the FBI."

Delgado obviously expected some sort of reaction, but when neither Brad or Logan showed any surprise, he rounded on Dex. "Have you kept your involvement in the investigation under wraps as instructed?"

Dex forced himself not to bristle at the imperious tone. "Gallagher and Ross have been brought in. That was a judgment call on my part. Merritt sent a PI to follow Meghan, and I wasn't about to jeopardize her safety by not utilizing every resource available to protect her. That means these guys. Keeping local law enforcement informed is smart, and helps keep her safe."

Delgado narrowed his eyes. "You're pretty protective of Ms. Bennett. First you insist on meeting without her, and now instead of working to build the case, I find out you've breached protocol to protect her. Are you keeping your relationship with her professional, Murphy?"

"I'm not with the FBI so that's none of your business."

"Which means you're personally involved. Son of a bitch." Delgado threw his pen down on the table with a clatter. "You know a relationship with the woman complicates matters by about a hundred fold."

"Like I said, none of your business."

Delgado drummed his fingers on the desk, then grabbed his pen. When he spoke again, his words were clipped. "I ought to haul your ass to jail for obstructing an investigation. Instead, I'm advising you to limit any personal involvement with Ms. Bennett."

Dex didn't say anything, and after a hard look, Delgado directed his attention to the other men. "I want to be clear that the FBI has jurisdiction and we will tolerate no interference from LEOs. We appreciate your support, but we'll be directing the investigation from here on out."

Brad raised a hand in a calming gesture when Logan opened his mouth in what Dex was sure wasn't going to be a polite response.

"We're not getting into a pissing contest with the FBI." Brad spoke with his usual, unperturbable calm. "But we do expect that the feds are smart enough not to overlook local support when it makes sense to use it."

"Done," Delgado said. "I'm making an official request that you turn over any evidence you have pertaining to the investigation."

"I will make sure that happens," Brad replied. "The most relevant evidence is a flash drive Ms. Bennett entrusted to me. If I turn it over to you, it's with the understanding that you will treat it with the utmost confidentiality and will respect that Ms. Bennett gave it to me voluntarily. The flash drive contains files she obtained from a personal computer in Merritt's possession."

"Agreed. Now that we've got that settled, let's move on. When Ms. Bennett and I meet, we will discuss a plan that I believe will, if successful, result in the arrest and prosecution of Julius Merritt."

Dex didn't like the sound of that. "I thought I was the bait to draw Merritt out."

"We're still working on that. If your assumption that Merritt is responsible for the burglary at your home and the shredded tire is correct, he's already breaking with his usual pattern of hiring underlings to do his dirty work."

"What are you talking about?" Logan interrupted, pausing with his cup midway to his mouth.

Delgado sat back in his seat. "Did Murphy tell you his history with Merritt?"

"Only that they had a run-in when Dex was a rookie."

"Yes, and when we put together what has happened to other people who have crossed Merritt, we found a pattern that looks a lot like attacks for the purpose of revenge. We were betting Merritt wouldn't be able to resist if he thought he could get back at Murphy, and we were right. He's gone beyond simple vandalism."

"What's he done?" Dex asked.

Delgado turned to him. "Do you remember a woman named Vanessa Martinez from a raid about three years ago? She was one of four young women from Honduras who had been sold to a pimp in Hollywood. You arrested the trafficker in a duplex in the Fairfax district."

Dex shook his head. "I remember the raid, but the name doesn't ring a bell."

"She's claiming that she was sexually assaulted by an LAPD detective after that raid."

"Fuck that."

"She says she's holding off naming the officer involved on the advice of her lawyer, but the implication is that it's you."

Declan narrowed his eyes. "What game are you playing, Delgado?"

Delgado smiled, a gesture that was of no comfort to Dex. "We have evidence that Merritt paid her to make the claim and, in addition to a cash payment, promised to get her American citizenship." Delgado twisted off the cap of a bottle of Coke before taking a sip. "Ms. Martinez is working for us. She was carrying a wire when she and Julius Merritt made the deal. We have a complete recording of the conversation. Now our tech guys are tracking the social media accounts that were spreading those claims for links to Merritt."

"Do you have anything to tie him to the attacks on any of the others who crossed him?"

"We're working on that, too. But what we really need is hard and fast evidence that Merritt fixed those test results to hide that his medical devices could kill people. Once we have that, the guy is cooked. We want to get him on both sides, the malicious personal attacks as well as the criminal business activities. If we do this right, he won't ever see the light of day again."

"That's all good, except that you want Meghan to get that evidence."

"We do. Even if what she got on the flash drive is solid, Merritt could argue that Ms. Bennett herself changed the records or tampered with the data. Until we get Merritt to admit to what he did, his lawyers have too good a chance dodging a conviction on reasonable doubt."

"Your plan sucks. I don't want her near the bastard." He knew his tone was hot, but the idea of Meghan going into a meeting alone with Merritt made him feel like a hard ball of ice had settled in his gut. "Merritt is unstable and he's already physically assaulted her. I don't want her alone with him."

"That's not your call, Murphy."

Brad's phone chimed and he picked it up to read the text. "That's Captain Morgan. He brought in Ms. Bennett to join us."

Dex swore under his breath. He had no doubt Meg would chew his ass for having the meeting without her. He needed a few more minutes with Delgado to work out a different plan, something that didn't involve Meg walking into danger facing a madman. Add that he hadn't told her of his own involvement with Julius Merritt, and Dex figured he was toast either way.

He wasn't wrong. The door opened and Meghan entered the room, her gaze meeting his with enough chill to give him frostbite. He caught the deliberate snub when she took the empty chair next to Logan rather than the one beside his.

Shit.

Chapter Fifteen

"Ms. Bennett, I'm Special Agent Esteban Delgado with the FBI. Thank you for agreeing to this meeting. Are introductions in order, or do you already know everyone in the room?"

"I know everyone." Meghan's cool tone matched her demeanor.

"Good, good." Delgado's jovial tone wasn't hitting the mark. "To bring you up to speed, my agency has reviewed the evidence and suspects it was Julius Merritt who broke into and entered the cabin that is in your late father's name, as well as vandalized Mr. Murphy's vehicle.

"We have verified that a vehicle owned by Merritt was spotted in a location near here shortly after last night's incident, and we have now verified that Merritt arrived at his Santa Cruz home in the early hours this morning. I am proposing that the FBI facilitates a meeting between you and Julius Merritt for the purposes of obtaining information that would be useful in his prosecution. We're looking for additional evidence that he knowingly marketed flawed medical devices that have caused bodily harm and even death, and purposefully misled investors in his company."

"Since Julius no longer trusts me, I don't believe he will willingly meet with me."

"I disagree. As you've probably observed, Julius Merritt is egocentric. He believes he is smarter than anyone else, and sees most everyone as an opponent or rival, and absolutely hates if someone comes out on top or defeats him. We have evidence that he has brought physical injury or financial ruin to people he perceives have somehow bested him. Our calculation is that his vanity and desire for revenge won't let him pass up the chance to meet with you if that opportunity was presented in the right way."

"How would I get the evidence you want?" Meg's voice sounded carefully controlled, and it was hard for Dex to get a read on what she was really thinking.

"You would meet him at his home, and wear a listening device that would allow agents in a surveillance vehicle to record your conversation."

Dex leaned forward in his seat. He kept his hands gripped around the arms of his chair to keep himself from reaching out and throttling the man. "No fucking way, Delgado. It's too dangerous. You've said yourself Merritt is a nutjob. He's already shown he's willing to use physical force against Meghan, and there's no telling what he'd do if he finds out she's wired."

Her deep blue eyes were glacial when Meg turned to face him. "You have no say in this matter, Declan Murphy. In fact, I'm not even sure why you're here."

"What did you do to piss her off?" Logan muttered in a quiet voice.

Sparing Logan a cool glance, she turned her attention back to Delgado. "Julius Merritt is unstable, and I don't trust him. If I show up at his house, I think he'll lose control. There's got to be another way. I'm not saying I won't help, but not with me alone with Julius. Beyond that, I should have asked my lawyer to be present today because it seems that if I were to agree to help the FBI, I should be able to negotiate for leniency on any charges that might be brought against me."

"We'll work on the plan so you don't feel vulnerable. But you've got to give us something if we're going to ask for charges to be dropped," Delgado argued. Dex didn't like Delgado's satisfied smile with the way the conversation was going.

"I texted Brenda Nguyen," Brad interjected. "She's Meg's lawyer," he said for Delgado's benefit. "She says she can be here in twenty minutes. Let's hit the pause button until she gets here so we can work out the details for Meg's cooperation."

"Great," Delgado said. "That will give me time make a call to confirm the Assistant U.S Attorney will be on board with making a deal, and he'll square that with the local DA in Santa Cruz"

They all stood, and Declan turned to block Meg's way. "Wait. We need to talk."

If looks could kill, he'd be lying on the floor, twitching. Meg's expression said she wanted to punch him in the throat if he stepped any closer. The others filed out of the room, and when she would have followed, he risked his life and snagged her wrist to keep her back.

She jerked her arm away. "Hands off."

"Look, I—"

"No, you look. You lied to me. We wanted to keep the little lady in the dark while the *menfolk,"* the word was said with a sneer, "decided what was best for her. Well, you know where you can stick your sexist attitude."

She tried to whirl away but once again he caught her wrist.

Her hiss of displeasure sounded like a snake ready to strike. "In case you haven't gotten the point yet, you no longer have the right to touch me. I said hands off."

He dropped her hand. "Would you listen for one damned second?"

"I don't have to listen. You lied to me."

"Yeah, I did, and I'm sorry. I wanted to check out Delgado before he got to you."

"So you had your cop buddy Bradley Gallagher set up the meeting with you instead of me, when I'm the one at the center of this? He's as sexist as you are."

"Don't blame Brad. I arranged to meet Delgado, and asked Brad and Logan to come. Brad's the one who wanted to bring you in." He paused, then decided he might as well say what he was thinking. "You're with me, Meghan, and I will do whatever it takes to protect you, whether you think that's sexist or not."

"Wow, we're together? That's quite an assumption. Get this straight, Declan Murphy. I don't need you to protect me. I make decisions for myself."

He knew he had to tread carefully. "In general, absolutely. But I know cops, and cops like Delgado have one goal, that's to nail the whoever they're after. That's a worthy goal, but sometimes innocent people get hurt along the way. I want to keep you from getting hurt."

"You could have explained all that instead of putting on the fake show and acting like you were going to hang out with your buds."

"If I had, would you have let me check out Delgado first?"

"No, but I wouldn't have been mad at you." Her eyes narrowed. "Back up a minute. You knew Delgado, but Brad didn't? Why is that?"

The wheels were turning, and he knew damned well she'd come to the obvious conclusion, a conclusion that would uncover another instance of him lying to her. The door opened, and the lady from the front desk announced that Brenda Nguyen had arrived.

Dex rubbed a hand over his face at the reprieve, and Meg left him with a furious expression.

***

After meeting with Brenda in Brad's office, Meg followed the others back into the conference room. She took a seat next to her attorney, and Declan moved to a chair next to her. Her emotions were all over the place where Declan was concerned. She would never allow a man to take choices away from her, but she'd be the first to admit that dealing with law enforcement and criminals was not in her expertise, so maybe Declan had a point. He'd gone about it poorly and she was still pissed, but she figured she'd let him know. But now she was suspicious that his involvement was deeper than he'd admitted to.

Delgado motioned to Brenda, who bent her head forward to hear what he had to say.

Minutes later, the agent addressed the group in a manner Meg found smarmy, like he was doing everyone a favor by talking to them. "It looks like we've worked out an arrangement. In exchange for Ms. Bennett's cooperation, the Assistant U.S. Attorney has agreed not to press charges on any of the possible counts against her involving Merritt, save for the disbursement of monies that she transferred from his accounts. That issue is still pending. The AUSA acknowledges that Ms. Bennett did bring relevant information to the Santa Cruz police, and is investigating why that wasn't acted upon. We've sent the data on the flash drive to an FBI analyst who has been instructed to get back to us as soon as possible."

Logan picked up his coffee and took a long sip. Meg had a sneaking suspicion it was to hide a grimace at Delgado's tone.

"We want to move swiftly on this while Merritt is still at his residence in Santa Cruz. Ms. Bennett," Delgado turned to Meg, "I would like to meet with you to review procedures and protocols, and any additional information to make this operation successful."

Before Brenda could delineate *their* plan, which provided that Meg would not meet Julius alone at his residence, Declan stated, "I'm going in with her." His firm voice brooked no argument.

Meg turned to face him, but he kept his gaze locked on the FBI agent.

"Think about it," Declan cut in when Delgado began to bluster. "Merritt searched the cabin. He already knows Meg and I are together." Meg barely refrained from kicking him under the desk at that statement. "We can use that. Every action Merritt takes is guided by his emotions. They're always on the surface. We know Merritt felt humiliated when I arrested him all those years ago, especially with all the added attention when that photo circulated, and was further embarrassed when it resurfaced again the following year, stirring the whole thing up all over again. With his history with Meghan and me, when we show up on his doorstep he's going to want to deal with us. His reaction will be emotional and that's good, because he'll slip up and say something damning."

Meg felt like the ground was shifting beneath her. "What are you talking about? You already knew Julius?"

He gave her a straight look. "Yeah." The shaky feeling increased at the flash of regret she saw in his expression.

"How are you involved with him?"

"I arrested Merritt when I was a rookie. He was drunk and acting like an idiot, then blamed me for arresting him."

"There's more to it than that," Delgado interrupted. "Photos of the event were all over the papers. We didn't have social media back then like we do today, but I think every other person in America saw the photo that was dubbed 'The Hunk and the Drunk.'"

"Except me," Meg muttered.

"Were you the hunk or the drunk?" Logan asked Declan with a crooked grin.

He closed his eyes and rubbed the bridge of his nose. "The point is, Merritt was pissed with the attention because it made him look like the ass he is. He tried to clean up his image, but then it was all stirred up again a year later."

"You'd better explain," Brad prompted.

"Right," Declan sighed. "I arrested Julius Merritt for public intoxication and vandalism. My partner and I had taken a midnight call about an out-of-control party at a frat house near the USC campus. We got there and found a large number of inebriated college kids, some engaging in criminal behavior. When I spotted Merritt, he was near naked and pissing through the open window of a neighbor's car. The neighbor who had called the cops because of the party."

He continued, "In addition to underage drinking, a girl had passed out and her friends were having to beat off the asshole frat bros who were trying to take advantage of her. Drugs and drug paraphernalia were present, and vehicles on the street sustained property damage caused by the intoxicated partiers scrambling to flee when the police showed up. Merritt was among the most obnoxious of the crowd. He'd managed to vomit on himself and had failed to zip his fly, then he resisted arrest, so he wasn't looking so good when the newspaper guy took the photo."

"I found the picture," Brad broke in. He'd been scrolling on his phone. "There's also the article from a year later. I'll airdrop them to those of you with iPhones."

After the break-in, Meg had decided there was no longer reason not to use her phone. She pulled it out and accepted the airdrop, then tapped open the photo app. The caption on the first image read "The Hunk and the Drunk—LAPD rookie Declan Murphy arrests USC student after drunken brawl." The photo showed a uniformed and clean-shaven Declan walking a handcuffed Julius Merritt to a police cruiser. The difference between the two men was glaring. Declan, chisel-jawed and serious—quite the young hottie, Meg had to admit—standing tall next to the unkempt and paunchy mess that had been Julius Merritt.

She scrolled to the next image, which was from a newspaper article. This one was titled "Hunk to the Rescue," and showed a shirtless Declan emerging from the surf towing two boys holding on to a long surfboard. According to the article, off-duty officer Declan Murphy, of the previous year's "Hunk and the Drunk" fame, had aided lifeguards when a group of young teenagers had become caught in a rip current off Huntington Beach. The article reran Declan's photo with Julius, and the reporter identified Julius Merritt as the "drunk," who'd made an effort to redeem himself, having graduated from USC and founded a company that made medical devices.

She caught Declan's gaze when she clicked off her phone. "Why didn't you tell me you knew Julius?" Meg spoke in a quiet voice, not quite able to prevent herself from revealing the hurt caused by the deception.

He turned his body toward her. "I'm sorry, I couldn't. I had agreed to work with the FBI before I'd met you, and they," he glared at Delgado, "made me swear to keep it from you."

"But you told Brad and Logan."

"Only when I thought you were in danger."

She looked away. She didn't want to have this discussion in front of the others, but she didn't like feeling like a fool. She'd trusted Declan.

Delgado cleared his throat to bring attention back to him. "I think your plan is flawed, Murphy. Merritt will be on guard if you're there. He may feel more comfortable if it's only Ms. Bennett and he'll be more likely to slip up. The FBI will be in a surveillance van parked within a quarter mile and with the capability of being at Merritt's home in seconds if there's a problem."

"No. I'm going in with her. Merritt is too volatile and that puts Meghan at risk."

Since Meg had no desire to confront Julius on her own, she kept her mouth shut.

"Ms. Bennett agreed to go in alone in return for dropping charges. That deal didn't include you, Murphy."

"Ah," Brenda cut in, "no, she didn't. Ms. Bennett asked to include me after you made your pitch, and she stated she wanted to work something out to get charges reduced. You told her you'd look into that. At no time did she agree to your plan."

Logan snickered. Brad kept his cool, calm reserve, and Declan grinned before saying, "It's on you, Delgado. Either I go in with her, or it looks like the lady is taking a pass."

"I think he's right," Brad interjected before Delgado could respond. "Meg will be safer if Dex is with her, and from what I've learned about Merritt, his ego won't let him pass up a chance to get at Dex, especially if he thinks he'll have the advantage."

Delgado's irritated expression returned. He must have banked on the bickering between her and Declan, because he asked the next question with the air of a man sure of her answer. "Do you want Mr. Murphy to accompany you when you confront Julius Merritt, Ms. Bennett?"

She didn't hesitate. "Absolutely. I want Declan with me."

Chapter Sixteen

Meg sat in the passenger seat, listening while Declan communicated with the team in the surveillance van parked in front of them. While Declan had argued vehemently that he be the only one wearing the wire, the FBI agent had pulled rank, insisting they both wear the devices. Then there was an argument about the type of devices since Declan was concerned Merritt would scan them, and wanted the least detectable wire the FBI techies could get their hands on. He'd made a pitch to go in by himself. Delgado had shut that down, and by the time everything had been settled, she had the feeling Declan would be happy wrapping her in cotton wool and putting her on a shelf someplace where there was zero risk.

On the one hand, his protective streak made her feel safe, but on the other, she didn't want him trying to limit her actions because of perceived threats. If that wasn't contradictory, she didn't know what was. And after the meeting in Hangman's Loss the day before, she was even less sure of her relationship with him. Despite her growing feelings, she wanted a man who respected her to make the right decisions for herself, and who didn't treat her like something fragile and easily damaged.

After the meeting, they'd spent the afternoon in a disgustingly long briefing with Delgado, and neither of them had spoken much when they'd returned to the cabin. She'd gone up to bed first and had chosen to sleep in the twin bed in the small bedroom. She'd tossed and turned, not able to get to sleep. About an hour after she'd gone up, Declan had climbed the stairs with his heavy tread. He'd paused outside her door, but then his footsteps had receded as he crossed the landing to his own room, and her heart hurt.

"We're good to go."

Meg gave a little jolt. She had been so deep in her thoughts she hadn't realized Declan had concluded his conversation. He started the engine on the dark sedan the FBI had provided, and drove along familiar streets. The blue water of Monterey Bay glinted between the twisted trunks of cypress trees, reminding Meg why she had loved living in Santa Cruz.

She drew in a steadying breath when he stopped the car alongside a stone wall a few yards before the gate to Julius's home. Her stomach clenched, and she wasn't too proud to admit that having Declan here lessened her scared-out-of-her-mind level of anxiety drastically.

He reached out to grasp her hand, and she didn't bother resisting when he brought it to his mouth to brush warm lips across her knuckles. "It's not too late to change your mind."

"The guys in the van can hear everything you're saying, you know."

"Don't give a damn. If you don't want to go in there, you don't have to. I don't think they could get any charges against you to stick, regardless."

She was already shaking her head. "Julius has hurt too many people. If what I'm doing results in him paying for what he's done, and prevents him from doing more harm, then I'm going to do it."

He held her gaze as if he was looking for a way to talk her out of doing this, then he released her hand, put the car into drive, and approached the gate.

Meg's guess that Julius wouldn't have changed the code was about to be tested. For all his "savvy," he believed himself invulnerable and was lazy about rotating his codes. She rattled off the numbers, and when Declan punched them in, the gate swung silently open. First hurdle passed.

He steered the car along the wide curving drive lined by queen palms to the palatial home. A long, arched portico stretched across the front, providing a shady entrance to the white stone façade. He gave a low whistle as he pulled to a stop. "Got himself some prime property, didn't he?"

The clutching in her stomach kept Meg from responding. Now that they were at the house, her nervousness had her wishing she hadn't eaten the fish tacos they'd lunched on with the FBI crew.

Declan took her hand as they approached the wide double doors, his thumb stroking over her knuckles. Meg pushed the doorbell made of elaborately worked bronze in the shape of a dragon. Declan dropped her hand and she took a step back when she heard footsteps approaching the door from inside.

***

Dex had a pretty good mental image of the inside of Merritt's house from the description Meg had given. Tri-level and built against the side of a bluff, entertaining was done on the middle level where the kitchen was located and the dining area opened to a wide deck and pool. Bedrooms were upstairs, and the lower level held the "man-cave," a concept Dex had always viewed as inherently selfish. He could see the toys she'd described in his mind's eye—the full-size arcade games, a pool table, the big-ass flat screen that took up most of the wall with accompanying theater seats, and a bar stocked with almost any alcoholic beverage one could desire.

He spotted the cameras in the entryway that announced their presence. The lock clicked and Julius Merritt swung the door open, a man in his mid-thirties who looked fifteen years older. He wore baggy pants with an oversize shirt left untucked but still not able to hide a substantial belly. A chunky gold necklace was the only indication of the wealth he possessed. Money hadn't brought good health, though. The bloodshot eyes, sagging jowls, and gray complexion gave evidence of a man who was paying for a lifetime of overindulgence.

His face twisted into a sneer. "What the fuck do you two want?"

Before Meg could follow the script laid out by Delgado, a script Dex thought gave Merritt too much wiggle room, he responded abruptly, "We want our property back."

"I don't know what the hell you're talking about."

"Sure you do. You broke into my cabin and stole our computers. We want them back."

"Your cabin?"

For a moment, Dex thought he would reveal that he knew about the cabin, perhaps that he'd been in it.

It took several seconds before Merritt continued, though on a different track. "Seems to me you've come down in the world,

Murphy. You crapped out as a cop, and I'm surprised you have the balls to come here without backup. Is this the best you can do these days? Hide behind a woman's skirts while you try your hand at extortion, or whatever it is you're doing here today?" In a mercurial mood shift, he threw back his head and laughed. "What the hell, come on in. Search the place if you like. You won't find shit, because I didn't take your fucking property."

Merritt held open the door with a grand gesture and Dex stepped in first, eyes scanning for any hint of danger. Merritt ignored Meg, focusing instead on Dex, which was exactly as he wanted it.

He caught the skunky odor of marijuana and figured that explained Merritt's red eyes, disheveled appearance, and the fact he didn't even ask to search them to look for a wire. Dark wood flooring, polished to a gleam, stretched through the open architecture to the far wall where French doors opened onto a deck. Dex could see the sparkle of the bay beyond.

"Come, let's sit and behave like civilized beings. You are capable of that, aren't you, ex-cop Murphy? Doesn't that eat at you, that you couldn't handle the job? I heard you got shot. Does it still give you pain? I hope to god it does, and for the rest of your life. That would mean there's justice somewhere in the universe."

Merritt turned to lead them into the living room, and Dex scrutinized the asshole's clothing. The elastic of Merritt's pants was too loose to be hiding a firearm in his waistband, and there was nothing heavy in his pockets.

He led the way to a sunken sitting area where a white leather sectional sat on a white rug, and a glass coffee table held a bunch of white flowers. Maybe white on white was a thing. Framed paintings, the modern crap that gave Dex a headache, hung on the walls to add discordant splashes of color, as did the hunks of multicolored glass displayed on most flat surfaces. He figured those were art, too, but they looked like large blobs of glass.

Merritt took a seat at one end of the couch next to an end table, draping an arm along the back. "I must admit seeing you at my door is unexpected, though I'm not surprised someone stole from you. That tells me you're careless, and either you're an easy mark or you have enemies. But I can't believe you actually thought *I* was the thief. I could buy laptops for every homeless drug addict in this city and not feel the pinch."

"I never said you stole laptops, I said computers," Dex remarked. He remained standing while Meg sat at the opposite end of the couch from Merritt.

"Of course, they were laptops. I know Meg has a laptop, and no one steals desktops. You're not dumb enough to think you can trip me up on something as inane as that, are you, ex-cop Murphy?"

Merritt seemed to tire of his game and didn't wait for an answer. Dex eased closer to Merritt when he turned his attention to Meg. Dex wanted to be sure his wire picked up the conversation, and he flat-out didn't trust the fucker not to do something stupid.

"Meg, you've been quiet. Are you letting this Neanderthal speak for you? I thought you were smarter than that. I must say, I'm disappointed that you deceived me. I'm too trusting, I guess. Did Murphy set you up to steal from me?" Bloodshot eyes surveyed them both.

Meg cleared her throat. "I didn't know Declan when I worked for you. That doesn't matter, though. In addition to wanting our laptops back, I've come to make a deal."

"A deal? You want to make a deal with me?" A flush spread across Merritt's cheeks as his voice rose in pitch. "You stole from me. You took files, and you stole investor money. I need that money to save lives." Meg had come up with the idea of proposing a "deal," sure that it would push Merritt's buttons and make him more likely to react emotionally, and with less restraint on what came out of his mouth. It seemed to be working.

"Your devices are killing people, not saving lives. You know that, otherwise you wouldn't have altered the research data."

Merritt heaved an angry sigh and the hand on his lap clenched, making Dex wonder if Meg had come on her own, would Merritt have used that fist. "I thought you understood. Sure, a few people will die after getting the heart device. They would have died anyway. There are so many others whose lives are being saved because of my invention."

"Aren't those patients entitled to know the risks before the procedure?"

"People are too emotional to make rational decisions when facing a health crisis. I did what I did for the good of mankind."

That sanctimonious tone irritated the hell out of Dex, but he had to hand it to Meg, she was good. She nearly had what they needed already.

"I guess you're right, Julius, I don't understand. What you did feels criminal to me."

Merritt's agitation eased a bit. He sat forward, his tone turning professorial. "Maybe I need to make this simple. If patients, or even their doctors, looked at the data as presented by the research group, the conclusion might be that having the device implanted is too risky. By adjusting the data, I'm merely helping them to arrive at the correct conclusion, which is that the odds of living for three years post-operation are high enough to justify the risks of the procedure."

Bingo. That was enough to get a conviction. Now they could get out and let the FBI do its job.

"I guess I understand now." Meg's meek tone seemed to placate Merritt.

"Good, I sometimes forget that common people can't keep up with me."

Dex barely quashed the urge to roll his eyes.

"But it's still dishonest, and you certainly make more money by manipulating people to have the device implanted." Meg needed to let it go, and Dex had to get her out of there before Merritt turned violent.

"The nuances of the argument are obviously lost on you." Disapproval dripped from Merritt's words, his hands clenching into fists. "Meg, I want you to return what you took from me, or I'll be forced to go to the authorities."

While Merritt was becoming increasingly agitated, Meg's voice remained calm. Only the fingers knotted in her lap gave away her tension. "I don't think you'll call the police," she stated. "Regardless of how you spin it, what you've been doing is criminal, and when I turn the flash drive over to them, you'll be arrested. I didn't fully realize how much of what you were doing was illegal when I was working for you, but having gone over the files more carefully, I know more now. Making a deal with me is a lot safer for you than the alternative. If you want any of those records back, you'll have to make that deal."

Merritt's forced laughter held no humor. "Oh, I get it. That was your plan all along, wasn't it? Gain my confidence, get your hands on files that are important to my business, and then use them to extort money from me. I must say, I'm impressed you're that clever." He turned his attention to Dex. "I should have known you were corrupt. All cops are corrupt. But you've made a big mistake in picking me as your mark. I haven't done anything wrong."

"Then you won't care if we turn over what we've found to the FBI." Dex gave him a grim smile.

"Go ahead. All that will do is expose your attempt to defraud me."

Declan wanted to find a way out of the situation before Merritt did something stupid.

"I'm curious, Meg," Merritt asked. "How did ex-cop Murphy convince you to play your part in this fraud?"

"It doesn't matter how the plan came about, the point is where we're at now."

"You already stole money from me. Wasn't that enough?"

"That's why we're here, because it wasn't hardly enough. I realize I should have taken more."

"How do I know you'll be honest with me? You could be conning me all over again. Like I said, you can give the police the files, but it's much simpler to give them back to me."

Meg pulled the lanyard holding the flash drive from under her shirt. "What you want is on this device. If you give back our laptops, plus a million dollars for our trouble, I'll give you the flash drive. I know what's in your bank accounts. With a little shifting of funds, you can get your hands on a million dollars in five minutes."

"And if I don't?"

"I'll send the files, anonymously of course, to the appropriate law enforcement agency."

Despite the cool breeze flowing in from the open French doors, sweat was beading on Merritt's forehead. "You're asking me to trust someone who has already proven to be untrustworthy."

"I don't think you have any choice but to trust me, Julius. I know you manipulated data to make your medical devices appear more successful than they really are, and you used that altered information to entice investors. How could you do that when you know people were dying because the medical devices were failing?"

"I knew nothing of the sort. I have no idea what you're talking about."

"I think you do."

The expression on Merritt's face turned cagey. "Okay, let's say for argument's sake you have evidence that I changed a few numbers here and there." Dex wondered if Merritt realized he was hedging on his previous admission of "adjusting the data." Cagey bastard. "Not saying that I did, but *if* I had, don't you think I'd be smart enough to hide my involvement? Why, I bet I could change those numbers and implicate my assistant to make it look like she altered the data and sent that information to potential investors." He let that sink in. "So you see, Meg, if you take that flash drive to law enforcement, it's you who will end up in prison, not me."

"Think you've got it all figured out, don't you, Merritt?" Dex couldn't have kept the disgust out of his voice if he'd tried.

"That's right, Murphy. You're a thug, same as you've always been. All brawn, no brain. It's the brilliant people like me who make things happen in this world."

"Is that right?"

"That's exactly right."

"Except you weren't brilliant enough to prevent Meg from taking all the files she wanted to copy."

Despite his bravado, Merritt was continuing to perspire, his white shirt sticking to his body, damp spots evident under his arms. "All Meg has proven is that I can't trust anyone. I haven't done anything wrong, and she's continued to try to take advantage of me."

"I think you're bluffing, Merritt. I think you're freaked because you know what Meg has on that flash drive, and you're petrified she'll turn it over to the cops."

"In case you're interested," Meg cut in, "I've arranged to have a duplicate of this flash drive sent to the FBI at seven o'clock this evening unless I give the order to stop the transfer. If anything happens to me, that information goes to the feds."

"I'm done talking to you." Merritt threw up a hand. "I should have done better research. I relied on employees to look into your background, and they obviously didn't do a thorough job. But the second you landed at that cabin, I figured you'd joined forces with this idiot." He indicated Declan.

"And how is that?"

"That cabin is in your dearly departed father's name, and a little digging came up with the fact that your father had been a cop."

"So?"

For the first time since they'd arrived, Dex felt uneasy.

"I'll tell you. That's how I knew you and Murphy are in this together. Your father was an LAPD captain, in charge of the division Murphy was assigned to. They knew each other, so it wasn't much of a jump to figure you also knew Murphy. I've waited a long time to pay this asshole back for trying to humiliate me. Now's as good a time as any."

In the instant of humming silence when Meg turned questioning eyes on Dex, Merritt reached for the end table. In a quick movement, he yanked open a drawer and pulled out a small, snub-nosed revolver.

"Gun," Dex yelled for the benefit of the feds in the van, then launched himself across the ten feet separating him from Merritt.

The impact sent both men tumbling over the back of the sofa, Dex grasping the hand holding the gun. Merritt's head hit the floor with a solid thunk and the gun went spinning across the gleaming wood. Dex heaved Merritt onto his belly with his hands wrenched behind his back. Meg scooped up the revolver and moved far enough away that there was no chance he'd grab the gun if somehow he escaped Dex's hold.

***

Heavy footfalls sounded and Meg rushed to the door to open it for the team who had been in the van. Four men, guns drawn and wearing bulletproof vests with "FBI" emblazoned on the back in block letters, surged past her. The last one across the threshold was Delgado. Once they saw that Merritt was in custody, they holstered their weapons. An agent passed Declan handcuffs, and he snapped them around Julius's wrists and hauled him to his feet.

Meg passed the gun to Delgado, who discharged the bullets before dropping the weapon and ammunition into evidence bags. The entire scene took on a surreal atmosphere. She'd lived in this house, she'd known Julius for almost a year, and now she'd played a part in his arrest. She wasn't sure if they'd gotten enough from him to make the best case, but that was up to the prosecutors to figure out.

Hoping to calm the tight spring of tension coiled inside her, Meg slipped into the kitchen and out through the open door to the deck where she leaned against the rail and took in the view of the ocean.

A long V of pelicans flew past, their awkward bodies rising and falling with the beat of their wings. As her emotions zinged along her nerves, thoughts pinballed through her brain. Declan had lied to her. From the beginning, he'd lied. He'd fudged about meeting with Delgado, and even after she'd told her whole long story about why she was on the run, Declan had kept his relationship with Julius a secret. Now she'd learned he and her father had been in the same division in the LAPD, never mind that her dad had been Declan's captain. She wondered how many more lies she'd discover.

Voices rumbled from inside the house, Delgado's carrying the loudest, informing someone they'd obtained a search warrant. That was that. Julius would be charged, and in all likelihood end up in jail.

Meg pulled in a deep breath of salt-tinged air. Now it was time for her to figure out the next phase of her life. She'd have to deal with the consequences for taking the investors' money and disbursing it to women through microgrants. Brenda Nguyen had suggested a strategy for coming away from that without being charged, and Meg had given the lawyer the go-ahead to see what she could do.

Once the house was cleared by Delgado's team, Meg went to the rooms that had been hers while living with Julius Merritt that still contained her things. She pulled a duffel bag from the closet and began carefully folding her clothes and placing them in the bag. She slipped into the kitchen to retrieve gallon-size zip bags. Declan was on the back deck, deep in conversation with one of the FBI agents who'd been in the surveillance van. She returned to the bathroom to gather her toiletries. At least wherever she ended up, she'd have her own shampoo and skin care products. Placing the sealed zip bags in the duffel, she took a last look around the room, hefted the bag over her shoulder, and walked out.

Meg didn't want to deal with Declan. She sent a text to her mother, then checked in with Delgado. For now, he didn't need her. After declining his offer of a ride, she slid into the Lyft she'd ordered when it arrived at the front of the house.

Chapter Seventeen

"Where's Meghan?

The glint in Delgado's eyes instantly put Dex on guard.

"Your girl's gone."

"What the hell do you mean, she's gone?"

"She packed a bag and ordered a ride. Left about fifteen minutes ago."

"No way. You need her statement, you wouldn't let her leave."

"I have her cell number." Delgado shrugged. "She's an adult. She wanted to leave. I didn't have any reason to stop her."

Dex battled back the urge to slam a fist into the wall. Her expression when Merritt had dropped the bomb that Roy Evans had been Dex's captain haunted him. He'd fucked up big time, and he needed to fix it.

"Do you know where she was going?"

Delgado shrugged, the gesture telling Dex as clear as words that Delgado wouldn't be any help.

"Shit. How about at least her phone number. Come on, Delgado, you owe me. If Merritt had pulled that gun with Meghan here on her own, she'd have been hurt, or worse, and you'd be explaining to the director how using her had put her in danger."

"You're a fucking bastard, Murphy."

"No doubt. Now give me her number."

Delgado did, and seconds later Dex was impatiently waiting for the call to go through.

"Hello?"

The knots that had a strangle hold on his heart loosened marginally when he heard her voice.

"Meghan, it's me." Dead air greeted that statement. "Don't hang up."

"What do you want, Declan?"

"You."

Her quickly indrawn breath grabbed him by the throat. That he wanted her was the absolute truth. She'd feared she would fall in love with him, but he was the one who'd fallen, and hard.

"Listen to what I have to say. Please. Then if you decide you don't want to talk to me, I'll leave you alone. At least until I can figure out a way to be more convincing."

He'd been hoping for a laugh, some small indication of her softening. He got nothing, no reaction at all. He stepped out onto the deck and pulled the sliding door shut behind him. He had privacy, but the fog rolling in had the temperature dropping.

"Look, I know I blew it. I should have been honest with you from the beginning. I wanted to, but I'd already agreed to work with the FBI, and I couldn't jeopardize the operation."

"And it would have jeopardized the operation to tell me that my dad was your commanding officer? How is that, Declan? Maybe I can understand you holding back about your relationship with Julius. But not telling me there was more to the story than that Dad saved your father's life in Vietnam doesn't make sense." She paused. "Or did you make all that up about what happened in Vietnam?"

"I did not make it up. But Roy was my captain when I arrested Julius. I didn't want you to make the connection back to him."

"What you're saying is it was okay to lie to me."

"It wasn't okay, but it was necessary."

"So what now?"

"Where are you? I'll come get you."

"No. I need to think without you clouding my brain."

"Meghan, I want some time with you, time so we can get to know each other without the rest of this crap going on."

"The crap, as you describe it, is still going on. I can still be charged for taking the money, and at the very least, I'll have to testify against Julius if there's a trial."

"Let me come pick you up. We can go back to the cabin together. We'll figure it all out."

"No, I have to decide what it is that I want. I'll get in touch with you about a good time to pick up my car and get my things."

Before he could say another word, the connection went dead.

***

Meg kept a firm grip on Gertie's leash as her mother locked the back door of her little cottage. Sarah Bennett looked fit and trim in her stretchy leggings and hip-length windbreaker. Silver dramatically streaked her black hair held back with a headband that also protected her ears from the cold.

"Let's go, Gertie girl," Sarah called to the dog. The cottage was only four blocks from a path that would lead them through low grass and down the bluff, and then to the beach. Gertie wasn't one to walk sedately, and Meg had to keep a tight grip on the dog as the three of them took the wooden steps down the face of the bluff.

A stiff, bone-chilling wind made her glad for the gloves and her own headband. The cries of seagulls rose over the roar of crashing waves, pitched high above the barking of a pair of seals who had pulled themselves up onto a grouping of rocks. Once on the coarse sand, Meg unclipped the leash and Gertie bulleted along the shore, oblivious to the cold as she splashed in the surf.

Agent Delgado had messaged her twice. Since the FBI had her and Declan's recordings of what happened, Delgado didn't expect her to come in to give her statement until tomorrow. Meg was happy to take the reprieve.

Walking beside her mother, Meg turned her face into the sea spray. She had always loved the wildness of the California coast, but today she found herself missing the jutting granite peaks and tall pines of the Sierras.

Her mom had given her a refuge, a listening ear, and a little time to get her head together after the drama of the previous few weeks. In the two days since she and Declan had knocked on Julius's door, Meg had done nothing but think about her future. She was in love with Declan. She'd known days ago. She couldn't decide if that complicated or smoothed the way to figuring out if she wanted to pursue a relationship with him. She'd ignored his text messages and phone calls until they'd stopped coming. That had made her wonder if he was giving her space, or he'd given up on her altogether and gone back to the cabin on the other side of the mountains.

"Are you going to tell me what's bothering you?"

Meg eyed her mother. "I already told you."

"You told me about that horrible Julius Merritt. But he's not the one who put shadows in your eyes. I'm guessing that has more to do with the young man staying at your father's cabin."

Yeah, *him*. He was definitely the problem.

Meg dodged Gertie as she raced up to shake water from her fur.

Sarah stared out past the waves, hoping to spot a whale or dolphins surfacing, but was really waiting Meg out.

Finally, she shrugged and confessed, "I'm in love with him."

Her mom draped an arm across Meg's shoulders. "That, being the intuitive person I am, and one who knows her daughter, I already gathered. Does he love you?"

Meg poked the toe of her shoe into the sand to flip over a scallop shell. "I don't know. He seems to care about me, but love is a big step for anyone."

"Meg."

She glanced up at her mother's no-nonsense tone. "What?"

"Trusting men is hard for you, but not all men are like your father."

"That's not the issue."

"I think it's at least partly the issue. Roy wasn't the kind of father you needed and deserved. I raised you on my own, and I regret that you didn't have a good male role model. Don't let that keep you from being happy."

"Declan hasn't been honest with me."

"Sometimes people aren't honest for good reason, and sometimes they have issues of their own. All I'm saying is if he's a good man, this should be something you can work through."

Meg considered her mother's words as they walked side by side crunching along the rocky shore, the only people on the beach on this drizzly fall day. Gertie nosed her way through driftwood heaped by the tide until she found a stick to her liking, pulled it free, then pranced over to Meg with her prize clamped between her teeth. With careful deliberation she laid the stick on Meg's foot, then backed up several steps, eyes shining in expectation. Meg hurled the stick as far as she could. Gertie gave chase, splashing through the low rippling tide and sending sandpipers scurrying. They repeated the process at least a dozen times before Meg clipped on the leash for the return trip to the cottage. She still hadn't figured out what to do about Declan, but maybe it was time to call him.

With Sarah in the lead, Meg and Gertie climbed the bluff, following the path until sand gave way to concrete.

Meg knew Declan cared for her, and believed that he was a good man. Flawed, but who wasn't? What she didn't know was if he felt more than a transient "love the one you're with," or if they had the beginning of something that could stand the test of time.

"Looks like matters are going to come to a head sooner rather than later," Sarah murmured. Gertie let out a bark, pulling on her leash as Declan stepped from the 4Runner parked in front of the cottage.

Meg's heart lodged in her throat at the same time her stomach dropped to her knees, which nearly buckled at the sight of him.

Damn.

He wore a leather jacket over a dark maroon shirt, his dark hair tossed by the wind. With his thumbs tucked in the front pockets of his jeans, he looked exactly how the young man at the bar had described him—seriously badass.

And good enough to eat.

He directed his attention first to Sarah, holding out his hand. "Ms. Bennett, I'm Declan Murphy."

"It's Sarah, and nice to meet you, Declan." Sarah shook his hand. Gertie nosed between them, and Declan lowered his hand for the dog to sniff, then rubbed her head.

"Why don't you two go on in the house to get out of the wind," Sarah suggested.

Meg escorted Declan into the living room while her mother took Gertie around back to clean her up.

Meg had yet to say a word. That initial surge of emotion at seeing Declan had settled into an overall feeling of rightness. And there was her answer. If she was with Declan, all was right in her world, which was *not* how she wanted to feel. Two weeks ago she hadn't even known he was alive, and now her universe was out of whack if he wasn't in it. Unsettling to learn her happiness was tied to a man who was a stranger in so many ways.

Declan wandered the room, perusing the shelves displaying framed photos and small sculptures from a local artist her mother admired. He peered closer at a photo of Meg taken when she was in college, her arm wrapped around Sadie, the golden retriever she'd adored and who had passed away of old age.

Not able to stand the silence, she asked, "Why are you here?"

He turned to face her. "You weren't taking my calls."

"I didn't want to talk with you."

"I know."

"So you decided to show up anyway."

He looked down, and Meg had the feeling he wasn't as confident as he appeared. "I don't want to lose what we have, Meghan."

"What exactly do we have, Declan?"

He stepped closer to reach for her hand.

Meg backed up a step. "Oh no you don't. I know how you are. You get ahold of my hands and all the sudden I'm a hot mess of lust. Keep your distance."

"Hot mess of lust, huh? That's promising."

"Get to the point, Declan Murphy."

"The point is, Meghan Bennett, I'm in love with you."

She thought her heart stuttered to a stop. Apparently, he didn't need to touch her hands for her to be a hot mess. She opened her mouth, not sure what she was going to tell him, but he stepped closer and stopped her with a finger to her lips.

"Let me say this first." She nodded. "I'm sorry. I'm sorry that I wasn't honest with you before." Despite her earlier comment, or maybe because of it, he took her hands in his and brought them to his lips in a gesture that was becoming endearingly familiar. "I need to work on being more open. That doesn't come easy to me."

He lowered his head for a moment before returning his dark gaze to her face. "I want us to be together, and I'll do whatever it takes to make that happen." He kissed her knuckles, looking suddenly unsure, perhaps not able to read that Meg was well on her way to that hot mess. His voice was gravelly when he spoke. "You said once that you thought you could fall in love with me. Is that still true, or have I screwed things up too badly?"

Meg wasn't someone for throwing caution to the wind, she tended to hold back, think things through, rein in impulses, then reexamine to make sure she knew her mind. But not this time. Not with this man.

Freeing her hands from Declan's, she reached up, her arms encircling his neck as she pulled him flush against her body. "I love you," she whispered in his ear.

His arms clenched around her and pressed her against him. She could feel the tension drain from his body. "God, Meghan, I thought I'd lost you."

They stood for a long moment, her head tucked under Declan's chin as he held her close, and Meg let the sensation of utter peace settle over her.

The scrambling clatter of toenails on the wood floor announced Gertie moments before a wet dog nose was thrust between them.

"Sorry. She got away from me." Sarah stepped in from the kitchen as Meg stepped back from Declan's embrace.

"Declan," Sarah asked, "will you be joining us for lunch?"

Chapter Eighteen

Dex turned off the highway to take the narrow two-lane road into the town of Hangman's Loss. Meghan stirred in the passenger seat beside him. She'd been sleeping for the past hour and now blinked her eyes open. After having lunch with her mother, he'd accompanied Meg to the FBI to give her statement then they'd left for home. The quiet drive had given him time to think, to plan. To hope. And since he couldn't see a reason not to, he decided to lay it all out.

"You awake?"

"Hmm." She didn't say anything for a moment, then nodded. "Yes." She sat up in her seat and peered out her window. "Oh, look at all the holiday lights. It's beautiful."

With Thanksgiving only days away, the town of Hangman's Loss had decked itself out for the holiday season with tiny white lights sparkling from lampposts, trees, and the eaves over the boardwalk. At close to midnight, the temperature on the dash read twenty-eight degrees, and fluffy, white flakes drifted from the sky.

He pulled the car over to park on the deserted street. They both had warm coats, so he guessed they wouldn't freeze.

"We're stopping here?"

Nerves had him jiggling his keys before taking a deep breath. He could do this. "Yeah."

Stomach churning, he pushed out of the car, slamming the door shut behind him. He circled to the other side to open the passenger door. Meg looked at him like he'd taken a crazy pill. Even knowing he could end up looking like an idiot, he pressed on.

Grabbing her hand, he pulled her from the car, then looked around somewhat desperately. He should have thought this through to ensure the result he wanted. The tall pine would work as a backdrop. A bench sat nestled against the trunk and the light dusting of snow made the white lights glow. He led her to the tree, then stood holding her hands, her expression puzzled.

That she would be with him standing under a tree in town in the middle of the freezing night despite her confusion, that when he looked at her he saw his future, told him he was making the right decision.

Their breaths combined to form puffs of vapor between them while silent white flakes landed in her hair. "God, you're beautiful. Okay, I can do this," he muttered to himself. Then the thought struck that he was missing a key element. He didn't have a ring. Damn it, why hadn't he thought of a ring?

"Declan, are you okay?"

"No, I'm not okay. I'm an idiot."

"Were you wanting to find someplace to get something to eat? Maybe the pub is still open."

She didn't have a clue what was in his head. He should have done this better. He thought the lights added a romantic element, but the freezing temperature probably cancelled that out. The hell with it.

"Marry me."

She brought up her hands to cover her mouth, eyes wide. Not sure if her stunned reaction was a good sign, he pressed on. "It's soon. I know that. And we have a lot to learn about each other, but I love you. I want to spend my life with you. Dammit, I'm messing this up."

He dropped to one knee. "Meghan Bennett, I love you. I want us to spend our lives together. Will you marry me? I'll get you a ring, whatever you want, but until—"

She pressed her hand to his lips to stop his babbling. "Yes."

"Yes? You'll marry me?"

"Yes, I'll marry you."

He surged to his feet, catching her up against him to swing her around.

He held her close as the tightness in his chest eased.

***

Meg sat at the small dining table in the tiny kitchen in their cabin, sipping her coffee. The light through the window was dazzling as the morning sun reflected off the night's light snowfall. She was going to marry Declan. Her mother had been happy for her, and she'd call her friend Andrea later. But for now, she hugged the knowledge close. Out of the grief and danger of the past several months, this one beautiful thing had happened. She had found the man who was right for her, who complemented her perfectly, who made her feel whole.

Earlier she'd awoken to a thudding sound and, peering out the second-floor window of the cabin, had spied her man, dressed in snow boots and a heavy wool shirt, wielding an axe. The pile of cleaved logs in the wheelbarrow told her he'd been at it for a while, and didn't he look yummy in a rough, mountain-man way.

Now the low rumble of his voice carried from the porch where he'd been stacking the chopped wood until his phone rang. His voice became more heated, making her think the conversation must have something to do with Julius, or possible charges against her. She wished she could have had a bit more time with Declan before the realities of the world burst their little bubble of happiness.

He swung open the door and came in from the cold, a scowl on his face. He shoved his phone in his pocket as his gaze sought out hers. He paused, seeming to make a conscious effort to relax. "Good news first."

"Okay. Hit me."

"The investors whose money you, let's say, redistributed, have agreed not to pursue charges against you. Instead they'll take the positive publicity of having made the microgrants to the organizations you sent the money to."

"Really?" Relief flooded through her, making her a little dizzy. "You were right all along. I'm not going to jail."

"You're not going to jail," he agreed.

"Okay, so what's the bad news?"

"They're releasing him."

"Who? Julius? How can that be?"

"That was Delgado. Merritt made bail. The AUSA was vehement against release, but Merritt's lawyer made the usual arguments—ties to the community, no priors." She raised her brow. "The college arrest was too long ago and too small to matter." Declan sighed.

"The judge set a high bail, but Merritt posted. He has the collateral in that house alone. He walked free an hour ago."

"Are they crazy? He's a threat to the community he's supposed to have ties to. He tries to get revenge against anyone who crosses him. Didn't the AUSA point that out?"

Declan held his hands in front of the fire crackling in the fireplace. "That was my question. Apparently, they haven't indicted him for those 'accidents.' They still don't have enough evidence. Plus, Delgado says he got himself a slick attorney who's claiming Merritt was framed by an out-of-control federal agency."

Meg let the ramifications of what Declan was saying sink in. The feeling of security she'd enjoyed since Julius's arrest had disappeared in the blink of an eye.

"Were there conditions for his release?"

"Yeah. He had to turn over his passport, plus any weapons. The FBI took possession of the gun he had the other day, and they didn't find any others in the house or his vehicles when they conducted their search, but it won't be hard for him to get whatever he wants on the black market without going through a background check."

"Are there travel restrictions?"

"He's not to leave the state. Which means we need to be on guard until he's back behind bars. Is that clear?"

"You think he's going to come here."

"I know he will. Delgado says the FBI will keep an eye on him, but they can't do that indefinitely. We need to be careful."

***

Despite the nagging worry about Julius, the next few days passed with her surrounded by a love Meg had never before experienced. She and Declan made love on the couch and then talked. They made love in the shower, and then talked. They made love more times than she thought imaginable in that big bed of his, and then they talked. To say she enjoyed Declan was an understatement. His incredible body and stamina were a wonder, and she found his dry sense of humor and quick intelligence a perfect match to her own. None of this was really a surprise; he'd hinted at those traits already.

But what Meg never expected was being loved by Declan Murphy was an intense and exhilarating experience. Intense, thoughtful, and so totally into her, down to her bones, she knew their souls were weaving together in a way time couldn't erase.

Yesterday, he'd taken her to a jeweler in town where they found a simple, traditional engagement ring with a beautiful pink diamond, and picked out the matching wedding bands. After that, whenever he held her hand, as was his habit, he would rub a finger over the ring, lovingly and possessively.

They were invited to Thanksgiving dinner at Brad and Emma's log cabin house near the lake, and no sooner had they arrived than Maddy, with an infant on her shoulder, marched Meg into the open kitchen area.

The aroma of roasting turkey competed with cinnamon and pumpkin as Maddy called out, "Attention, ladies." Emma, Dory, Maddy's cousin Eva, and an older woman holding a dark-haired toddler who Meg assumed was Owen all turned their heads.

She felt a little exposed when Maddy held up her hand and the engagement ring gleamed under the rustic light fixtures. "Our friend Meg is engaged."

"Declan proposed. Oh, I was sure he would," Emma cried, reaching out to give Meg a congratulatory hug. "He seems so much happier since you came. You'll be good for each other."

Dory held her hand over her heart. "Oh, that's wonderful. Did he get down on one knee?" At Meg's affirmative, Dory let out a heartfelt sigh. "That's so sweet."

The older woman set the toddler down on wobbly legs, then straightened to examine the ring. "That's a lovely ring. Meg, I'm Trish, Bradley and Madison's mother. Congratulations, hun. Declan is a good man."

A timer went off at the same time the back door opened. Trish prepared to pull the turkey from the oven as Brad and Logan trooped in, Logan holding a bundled baby like a football. "Diaper change time," he announced.

"Mason needs a change, too. I'll take them upstairs," Maddy told her husband.

"Nope, the men have got this one." He gathered his infant son, and with a baby on each shoulder, headed to the living room. "Dex," he called out, "you're gonna have one of these someday, so here's your first lesson." Declan's deer-in-the-headlights look didn't stop Logan from passing him a baby.

A charming, cute firefighter introduced as Diego came in the kitchen. He slid an arm around Eva's waist as he snagged a carrot from a veggie tray. He whispered something in her ear that had her tipping her head to rest on his shoulder. Owen tugged on Diego's pants and raised his arms.

Diego scooped him up. "Come on, little man. You can help me set the table."

"He's so good with babies," Trish commented, raising an eyebrow at her niece.

"He is," Eva replied. "But we're going to wait a couple years before we start a family. How about you, Meg? Will Dex be making use of Logan's lesson?"

Meg could feel the flush staining her cheeks at the speculative looks cast by the women. She held up her hands in surrender. "We haven't even planned the wedding, so don't start thinking babies."

The comment worked beautifully as a diversion, because talk turned to Eva's upcoming wedding. Meg was assured that the best place for a wedding in Hangman's Loss was at the resort Emma owned. From there, talk ping-ponged from wedding dresses, to catering, to the challenge of getting fresh-cut flowers. And through it all, Meg couldn't help being curious to know how Declan was doing changing a diaper.

***

"I don't have to go. We could stay in."

"Declan, go. Enjoy yourself."

Diego and Eva had decided to go traditional. Diego's bachelor party was an all-guy event being held at the Brew Pub. While strippers had been crossed off the entertainment list, alcoholic beverages would be plentiful, as well as pool and pinball tournaments.

"I talked to Delgado an hour ago. He confirmed that Merritt is at his home, so you don't have to worry."

"You're the one who's worried. I'm okay, Declan, I promise. I'm leaving in half an hour for Eva's bridal shower, so we're each having a night out."

"I don't see why they can't combine parties. That's what we should do. And why the hell is it called a shower? Does that make sense to you?"

"Not at all. Now go." She was kind of glad the bride and groom had decided on separate pre-wedding celebrations. Due to the events of the past few weeks, she knew the men in Declan's circle of friends a bit better than their partners, and was looking forward to the chance to spend some time getting to know the women better.

Meg understood she and Declan were on edge. Since Julius posted bail, updates from the police in Santa Cruz as well as the FBI had verified that he was confirmed to be at his residence. The FBI was monitoring him and reported that he'd been observed smoking joints on the back deck, entertaining women, driving back and forth in his Mercedes, and swimming laps in the pool.

She knew what was worrying Declan, because it was bothering her, too. It wasn't normal for Julius to act, well, normal. In all the time she'd been with him, she'd never seen him use the pool, and he'd never had women over. Smoking weed was typical for him, but the cops had also mentioned wine consumption, and Julius was more a beer or hard liquor kind of guy. She comforted herself with positive thoughts: he was on the other side of the state, and once the trial was over, she could forget ever having known him.

After locking the door behind Declan, she returned to the bathroom to put the finishing touches on her makeup. Her gift, a sampler of wine varieties from Napa Valley, had to be delivered, but Meg figured the bride-to-be wouldn't mind.

Wine…she paused, staring at her reflection as the facts flashed and coalesced. Julius didn't drink wine. She'd figured maybe he'd recently decided to switch, but now the truth was obvious. Grabbing her phone, she called Declan's number. When it went straight to voicemail, she tapped out a text message with trembling fingers.

Julius Merritt wasn't in Santa Cruz.

Chapter Nineteen

After pressing send, a sense of urgency pushed her to action. She would lock herself in the master bedroom and get the gun from the gun safe. She'd wait there until Declan returned. Buttercup leapt onto the back of the couch, reminding her of the fear for the calico's safety when Julius had broken in. She was reaching for the cat when the motion-activated light outside the back door flashed on and a chill snaked down her spine.

When she heard a soft clinking of metal at the lock, she grabbed the cat and had almost made it to the stairs when the kitchen door thrust open and Julius Merritt walked into the kitchen. Meg froze, clutching Buttercup to her chest. Julius shut the door quietly behind him, a move that set her nerves on edge.

He spied her, and his lips spread in a smug grin. "Honey, I'm home," he sang out. When she remained frozen, he cooed, "Meg, so nice to see you again. Aren't you going to welcome me with a hug?"

He'd dyed his hair a burnished red and had grown a scruffy mustache. Dark pants hung loosely on him, and he wore an overcoat that came to his knees. His shoes were better suited for a fashion statement than warmth. He seemed more alert, his eyes not as bloodshot as when she'd last seen him in Santa Cruz, though his skin still had the unhealthy gray cast.

Her heart thudded, fear growing tentacles to immobilize her as her mind raced to all the ways he could hurt her. She swallowed convulsively before speaking. "What are you doing here, Julius?"

"Is that any way to greet your old friend and boss?" He stepped further into the kitchen, gaze moving over the dishes on the drainer, the coffeemaker, the refrigerator with a photo of her and Declan together framed with a heart. Julius picked up a glass and nonchalantly tossed it into the sink where it shattered, making Meg jump.

"God, I love that sound." He ripped the photo from the fridge, sending the magnet flying. He stared at it for a moment, then turned on the burner on the stove. He held the paper to the flame. It caught, smoke rising as he dropped it into the sink to burn. A shrill tone sounded as the smoke alarm went off.

"Well, that's annoying." Julius waved a dishtowel at the alarm with a decided lack of urgency until the noise stopped.

Meg took a deep breath and forced back the terror brought on by his casual violence. She wouldn't survive if she allowed fear to paralyze her. She couldn't stand there and let him destroy things or hurt her. Trying to think rationally, she assessed Julius's physical capabilities. Maybe she could take him. She exercised, was physically fit, while Julius was overweight and out of shape. She watched him carefully, looking for the opportunity to act.

"A month ago I would have said this hovel is beneath you, but now that you've aligned yourself with ex-cop Murphy, I can see my assessment of your character was inaccurate."

Meg edged toward the front door. If she had a chance, she'd make a run for it. If she didn't, she'd fight.

Julius reached nonchalantly into his pocket to pull out a black pistol. Meg's heart skidded to a halt. Physically fit was no competition for a bullet. He turned the gun sideways to examine it with a slight frown, as if trying to understand how it had gotten into his hand. When he raised the gun, he pointed the dark eye of the muzzle at her.

"I always told myself I wasn't a murderer. Now I'm not sure why I held back. There's power in bringing another person's death." Meg had never before heard a more chilling statement.

He continued his perusal of the cabin, and Meg eased one foot behind her, slowly, cautiously, then the other.

"Were you going somewhere, Meg, dear? I can see you're dressed to go out. You'll have to adjust. I've been watching you and the asshole, Murphy, for the better part of two days. You've been holed up here like a couple of newlyweds. Screwing like rabbits, no doubt. You should know I'm disappointed in you. You could have had so much more, but instead, you chose to hook up with such an ignorant baboon."

Meg had an insane urge to laugh. Julius, with his delusions of self-importance, was comparing himself favorably with a man who had dedicated his life to protecting others.

Julius strolled into the living room, scanning the furnishings with the same disdainful expression. "You may have chosen Murphy, but he's not worthy." His expression turned sly. "I bet there are things about him, about his past, he hasn't told you. You can't trust him, he's a flawed individual. Let's sit down and we can have a nice chat while we're waiting for him to return and join us for the grand finale to the evening."

Buttercup squirmed in her arms, and Meg dropped her, noticing how Julius backed away when the cat darted in front of him. "When Declan comes back, he'll know something is wrong. He won't simply walk into a trap."

"Of course he will, that's what makes him such a Neanderthal. He has no sense of self-preservation." Julius let out a series of sneezes. "Fucking cat." He moved to the living room and flopped onto the couch, motioning to Meg with the gun. "Take a seat, and keep your hands where I can see them."

She followed his direction and sank into the green upholstered chair. Her brain had shifted to a hyperaware mode, constantly searching for something, anything she could use or do to give her an advantage.

Julius appeared to be brooding. "All right, get out your phone. We need to speed things up." He rose to stand behind her. "Text Murphy that there's a water leak under the sink that's spraying water all over the kitchen. That'll get him back here."

She texted the message and held it up for Julius to verify before hitting send. Julius returned to the couch.

"Would you like something to drink? Coffee, or beer?"

"Ha, and have you poison me again? You know I'm smarter than that. Do you realize I even contemplated selecting you to bear my child? What a mistake that would have been."

The bizarre nature of the comment threw her. "What are you talking about? I would never have a child with you."

He waved the gun in a negating gesture. "Of course, you would. I'm only telling you now so you know what opportunities you missed. You would have been compensated handsomely for producing my child, enough to make you financially secure for the rest of your life." He jiggled his leg restlessly. "But you chose to ally with ex-cop Murphy, and now you'll pay the price. How long will it take the washed-up cop to get back here?"

"Any second now."

Julius's fake laugh boomed through the cabin. "That was a test and you failed. Murphy was on his way to that bar where I had the pleasure of shredding his tire. Like I said, I've been here a few days."

Conversationally, as if they were old friends catching up, he continued talking. "I rented a cabin, much nicer than this one, by the way, and I've been hanging out at that same bar. In disguise, of course." He pointed to his hair. "Easy enough to learn about the plebeian bachelor party scheduled for this evening. There's a little surprise waiting for Murphy and his bros. Bonus for me is that most of the law enforcement and fire protection for this area, the asshole first responders, will be there. That's what gave me the idea. I'll get them all in one fell swoop. You know I'm efficient. Murphy, of course, will come home because sweet little Meg texted him, and will meet his end here."

Fear had Meg letting out a shuddering breath. It was worse, so much worse, that he planned something for Diego's bachelor party. Not letting her voice betray her fear, she hissed, "You won't get away with this, Julius. You should turn yourself in before you do anything that gets you hard time."

He bellowed out another laugh. "Do you want to know how smart I am? I'm a ghost, because no one will ever know I've been here." Meg realized Julius hadn't touched anything that would leave a fingerprint.

"But I want to share, and it doesn't matter if I tell you because shortly you'll be dead. Murphy will be dead. I'll return to my life and no one will be the wiser. Without your testimony and given my standing in the community, I expect no prison time. Maybe house arrest. But I digress. Ask me how smart I am, Meg."

He wouldn't kill her, she had to hold tight to that belief and push past the fear so she could be ready to take action. Keeping him talking, playing to his ego, were the first steps toward her survival. "How smart are you, Julius?"

"So smart I was able to fool the idiot FBI into thinking I'm still at my house in Santa Cruz. Want to know how?"

Having already guessed and acted on that gave Meg hope. She'd sent the group text before Julius had even walked through the door, but she played along. "How?"

"I paid my cousin Donny to pose as me. You remember him, don't you? I introduced you back when you first started working for me. What do you remember about him, Meg?" He questioned her like a first-grade teacher.

"That he looks a lot like you." Without any outward change in expression, Meg registered movement outside the darkened window of the cabin, nothing more than a slight shifting of shadow between the parted curtains. *Declan.* It had to be him. With the knowledge came the fear. Julius wanted to kill Declan, perhaps more than he wanted her dead.

Her firm belief that Declan would keep them both safe from harm was an act of faith.

"Not quite as good-looking, and certainly not as intelligent, but from a distance? We could pass for twins. I drove the Mercedes into town, met my cousin. We swapped clothes, and he drove back to my house and started living my life. It will be that easy to go back, because we'll do the switch in reverse. People see what they expect to see, and the FBI are easily fooled. It's an embarrassment, really." He sneezed, then wiped watering eyes on his sleeves. "Too bad we're not closer to that restaurant, I'd like to hear the big boom." He glanced at his watch. "Should be any minute now. If Murphy doesn't return, we'll have to assume he was caught in the explosion. If that's the case, I'll have to adjust how I deal with you." He shrugged. "Can't be helped."

"Why are you doing this, Julius?"

His gaze flew to hers, his face flushing bright red. "Because, Meg, people who cross me must pay." His tone was ragged, but evened out as he continued. "Do you remember me telling you how I liked to tinker? I taught myself to pick locks, hence the ease with which I got into this place. Another thing I taught myself? To make pipe bombs, which I find to be a useful skill."

A muffled noise came from the front porch at the same time as what sounded like a footstep from the second story. Julius jumped up from his lounging position on the couch, backing toward the fireplace. He stumbled over the cat bed, and frightened, Buttercup sunk her claws into his leg. When he screamed, she sprang away.

With a snarl, he aimed the gun at the cat. Meg launched herself as he pulled the trigger. The gunshot cracked through the air, and in that instant Declan leapt over the railing from the upstairs as the front door crashed open.

Meg collided with Julius at the same moment he began sneezing violently. She wasn't sure what her next move would be, but she didn't have to make the decision because thick strong arms hauled her back against a hard chest. A moment later she was spun to the side and she saw a big man with wavy brown hair wearing a marshal's star on his belt, kick Julius's feet out from under him as two large figures fell onto the still-sneezing man.

It was over in seconds. Brad had Julius on his stomach with his hands cuffed behind his back while Logan recited the Miranda warning. Jack pulled out the clip from Julius's gun and ejected the bullets, then placed everything in evidence bags. Buttercup, unscathed, sat on the back of the couch licking her paw and rubbing it over her ears.

Meg turned the moment she felt Declan's heat behind her. He wrapped her in his arms and murmured, "It's over, baby." He rested his cheek on the top of her head and repeated, "It's over."

Chapter Twenty

Dex stood up from the edge of a booth and shook hands with the burly man with the marshal's star on his belt that said, "Deputy US Marshal Linc Jameson. We didn't get to do introductions earlier."

"You're a friend of Logan's, right?" Dex asked.

"Yeah. I don't hold being ex-FBI against him." Linc grinned and Dex tipped his head in acknowledgment. Seemed general feelings about the feds were the same across the board. "A couple of days ago," Linc explained, "I finished an assignment with the Reno office and was taking some personal time. Logan wanted me to meet Maddy and show off their babies." Linc let out a laugh. "Wasn't expecting all the excitement."

"I'm grateful for your help, Jameson," Dex said as he clapped Linc on the shoulder.

"Not much for me to do, but I'll be glad to take that POS off your hands when my partner gets here in the morning."

"Not a moment too soon," Dex stated. Linc gave him a nod and then moved to the bar while Dex returned to his seat.

After a sneezing, cursing, whacked out of his head Julius Merritt had been secured in the Hangman's Loss jail, Dex, Brad, Logan, and Jack returned to the scheduled festivities. The two parties were combined, as Dex figured they should have been all along. Once the faulty pipe bomb had been found in the men's bathroom and dealt with, the women trooped to the Brew Pub for a combined bachelor party/bridal shower.

He wouldn't have minded staying at the cabin with Meg. Those long seconds on the upstairs landing of the cabin while he'd waited for the opportunity to grab Merritt had felt like a lifetime. Dex had relied on his training and had trusted the team he was with when what he'd really wanted to do was leap over the railing the moment he'd seen the gun. Watching while Meg was in mortal danger had shook him to his core. He needed to hold her, make love to her, prove to himself that she was truly safe. He'd never felt such bone-deep fear as when that gunshot had ripped through the cabin. Only now, more than an hour later, his system was leveling off after an adrenaline spike had nearly flattened him.

He scanned the bar before locking his gaze on his fiancée. He hadn't been looking for love. He never believed "the one" was waiting out there for him somewhere, he had figured that was nothing more than a romance-novel construct. Now he knew it was god's truth, and he had no idea how he'd lucked out in finding her.

After his divorce, he'd believed he'd make a good enough life, but had pretty much resigned himself to spending that life alone. Then, by some miracle, the woman who was perfect for him in every way had knocked on his door.

And hadn't gotten lost when he'd told her to.

Meg had placed her food order at the bar and stood chatting with Emma and Brad. Dex loved the way her face reflected her emotions, how her eyes lit with humor as she talked. The food was brought out, and she returned to their table with the huge platter of onion rings. She might as well have been the Pied Piper because the men and women he was beginning to think of as family followed her. Maddy was arm in arm with Dory. Brad, finally back from the police station, was holding hands with Emma. Logan, Linc, and Jack carried trays heavy with frosty mugs of beer.

Meg dropped into the seat next to Dex, settling into the curve of his arm. She tilted up her head to press a kiss to his jaw. "I'm glad we came. We both needed this."

"It's going to take me a while to get past that moment when I heard the gun go off." He tightened his arm. "But being here goes a long way."

And it did. The events of the evening were hashed and rehashed even as the soon-to-be-married couple was toasted, music played, and the pool and pinball competitions commenced. Brad, Jack, Logan, Declan—they had all received the group text Meg had sent. Dex had been so scared out of his mind for Meg, he'd scaled up the side of the cabin and climbed in through his bedroom window, while the other men had kicked in the front door. Now the federal marshals would take custody of Merritt. No way would that asshole be getting bail this time.

Dex admitted he took pleasure in hearing Brad and Logan agree that Agent Delgado would likely get slapped down by the FBI for allowing Julius Merritt to slip out of Santa Cruz and put Meg's life in danger once again.

The sounds of pinball machines competed with the crack of pool balls. Diego took the mic to sing a sappy love song for Eva, and had the table where a group of firefighters were seated, some still in their uniforms, razzing him.

Couples took to the floor when karaoke gave way to dance music. Logan grabbed Maddy's hand and led her onto the floor in a hot number that ended in a kiss fiery enough to scorch hair. Brad pulled Emma out onto the dance floor when the music turned slow, and Dex felt Meg's chest expand in a sigh.

"Dance with me?" he murmured in her ear.

At her nod, he took her hand, his thumb rubbing over the diamond on her ring finger as they made their way between dancing couples. He brought her hand to his lips and pressed a kiss to her knuckles before pulling her into a hold where they swayed to the beat.

"Marry me."

She tilted her head back. "You already asked me that. I think I said yes."

He grinned down at her. "You did say yes. I was making sure." He brought up his hands to frame her face, stroking his thumb along her jaw. "Christmas Eve is in two weeks."

She gave him a puzzled look. "True."

"My mom and stepdad will be here."

"Really? That's nice. I can't wait to meet them. Do you celebrate Christmas on Christmas Eve?"

"No. We could invite my sister and her family. Her kids are terrors, but we keep them anyway."

"That's commendable. I hope it's not too late to invite them."

"They'll make it when I tell them."

"Tell them what?"

"That there'll be a wedding."

Couples around them were swaying to the music, but Meg stood motionless, staring at Dex like he'd grown a second head.

"What do you mean? Diego and Eva's wedding is next weekend."

"It is. Meghan?"

The pulse in her neck fluttered under his thumb. "Yes?"

"Marry me on Christmas Eve."

He caught her when she leapt into his arms, her hands going to his cheeks as she rained kisses over his face. "I thought you'd never ask."

Come back to Hangman's Loss for Dory and Jack's story in
Clear Intent.

ABOUT THE AUTHOR

National Readers' Choice Award winner for her novel, *Solitary Man*, Diane Benefiel has been an avid reader all her life. She enjoys a wide range of genres, from westerns to fantasy to mysteries, but romance has always been a favorite. She writes what she loves best to read – emotional, heart-gripping romantic suspense novels. She likes writing romantic suspense because she can put the hero and heroine in all sorts of predicaments that they have to work together to overcome.

A native Southern Californian, Diane enjoys nothing better than summer. For a high school history teacher, summer means a break from teenagers, and summer allows her to spend her early mornings immersed in her current writing project. With both kids living out of the house, in addition to writing, she enjoys camping and gardening with her husband.

Diane loves hearing from her readers.

Website: dianebenefiel.com
Facebook: facebook.com/DianeBenefielRomance
Twitter: twitter.com/dianebenefiel
Instagram: diane_benefiel
Goodreads: goodreads.com/author/show/8075321.Diane_Benefiel
BookBub: bookbub.com/authors/diane-benefiel
Pinterest: diane_benefiel

If you enjoyed this book, please write a review. Our authors appreciate the feedback, and it helps future readers find books they love. We welcome your comments and invite you to send them to info@boroughspublishinggroup.com. Follow us on Facebook, Twitter and Instagram, and be sure to sign up for our newsletter for surprises and new releases from your favorite authors.

Are you an aspiring writer? Check out www.boroughspublishinggroup.com/submit and see if we can help you make your dreams come true.

www.ingramcontent.com/pod-product-compliance
Lightning Source LLC
Chambersburg PA
CBHW022112170626
46808CB00002B/700